D0962632

BOOK 6

# THE DEMONATA
# DEMON APOCALYPSE

## BY DARREN SHAN

1837

LITTLE, BROWN AND COMPANY
New York   Boston

Little, Brown and Company

Hachette Book Group
237 Park Avenue, New York, NY 10017
Visit our Web site at www.lb-teens.com

Little, Brown and Company is a division of Hachette Book Group, Inc.
The Little, Brown name and logo are trademarks of Hachette Book Group, Inc.

First U.S. Paperback Edition: May 2009
First U.S. Hardcover Edition published in May 2008 by Little, Brown and Company

First published in Great Britain by Collins in 2007

The characters and events portrayed in this book are fictitious. Any similarity to real
persons, living or dead, is coincidental and not intended by the author.

Library of Congress Cataloging-in-Publication Data

Shan, Darren.
Demon apocalypse / by Darren Shan.—1st U.S. ed.
    p. cm. —(Demonata ; bk. 6)
Summary: Grubbs Grady tries to resist his werewolf urges and evade the
eight-armed grasp of the demonic Lord Loss.
ISBN 978-0-316-00380-3
[1. Demonology—Fiction. 2. Werewolves—Fiction. 3. Horror stories.]  I.
Title.
PZ7.S52823De 2008
[Fic]—dc22

                                    2007035301


10 9 8 7 6 5 4 3 2 1


RRD-C


Printed in the United States of America

Also in

# THE DEMONATA

series:

For:

Bas — back with a vengeance!

OBEs (Order of the Bloody Entrails) to:
evil Elizabeth Eulberg — mistress of Duke's!
sinister Cynthia Eagan — steer clear of the spoon!

Prophet of doom:
Stella Paskins

Horsemen of the Apocalypse:
the Christopher Little seers

# PART ONE

✠     ✠     ✠

# BERANABUS

# THE SNATCH

✠     ✠     ✠

A DEMON shaped like a giant scorpion digs its stinger into a woman's eyes. As they pop, it spits eggs into the bloody sockets, then watches with its almost human face as the eggs hatch and wriggling maggots feast on her flesh.

Another demonic beast — it looks like a cute rabbit, though it has an ugly bulge on its back — vomits over a man and his two children. The acidic liquid sizzles and dissolves them down to the bone.

A third footman of the Demonata runs after a flight attendant. He has the body of a young boy but his head is larger than an adult's, he has a wig of living lice instead of hair, and fire burns in the holes where his eyes should be. He also has two extra mouths in the palms of his hands. The teeth of both are eagerly snapping open and shut as he chases the screaming flight attendant.

All the people on the plane are screaming — except those who've already been killed — and it's music to the ears of the demon master, Lord Loss. He hovers in the aisle, mouth twisted into a sad smile, red eyes distant. A few of his eight arms twitch in rhythm with the screams, like the conductor's of an orchestra. Then his eyes snap back into focus and he turns his gaze on me.

"You should not have humiliated me, Grubitsch," Lord Loss says, still furious about the time I beat him at chess. "You should have fought fairly, faithful to the spirit of the contest, and won or lost on merit alone. You ruined chess for me. For many centuries it was my only other source of joy. Now I have just the agony and torture of humans to keep me amused."

He slowly drifts down the aisle toward me, the strands of flesh that pass for his legs floating a few inches above the floor. The tiny snakes in the hole where his heart should be are writhing, hissing hatefully, spitting venom in my direction. Blood is flowing from the many cracks in his pale red skin. The holes above his upper lip — he has no nose — quiver wildly as he gleefully inhales the stench of terror from the doomed passengers. His dark red eyes are dilated with morbid pleasure. All eight of his arms are extended. Some of his mangled hands brush the heads and cheeks of humans as he passes, as if he is obscenely blessing them. The white-haired, pink-eyed, albino traitor, Juni Swan, is behind him, smiling serenely.

A woman clasping a baby falls to her knees in front of Lord Loss, sobbing painfully. "Please!" she cries. "Not my child. Have mercy on my baby. Don't kill him. I beg you!"

"Suffer to come unto me the little children," Lord Loss murmurs blasphemously, taking the baby with three of his hands. He strokes the boy's face and the baby laughs. Lord Loss passes him to Juni. "For you, my darling swan."

"You are generous to a fault, my lord." She smiles, then kisses the infant.

"No!" I scream. But it's too late. A moment later she tosses the grey remains of the baby aside, having sucked his fragile life from him. The child's mother chokes, eyes wide with disbelief and horror. Lord Loss bends and breathes in her sorrow, sighs contentedly, then moves on, leaving her to the lesser demons.

Sick with fear, I back away from the approaching demon master. There are several empty rows behind me — the other passengers have fled to the tail of the plane. Lord Loss makes a small humming noise. "At last you move. I thought I might wring no sport from you today."

"Leave them alone," I snarl, hands knotted into trembling fists. "It's me you want, so let the others go."

"I cannot do that, Grubitsch," Lord Loss sighs. "My familiars are hungry. I promised them food. You would not ask me to break my word, would you?"

"My master always keeps his promises," Juni chuckles.

I focus on her. The fair-faced but black-hearted cuckoo in the nest. She acted like my mother. I loved her. I let her steal me away from Dervish. And all the time she was plotting against me. "Harpy!" I sob. "What the hell are you — a demon in disguise?"

"I don't have that honor," she replies smoothly. "I'm merely a human like you. In fact, I'm from the same family tree, believe it or not. But unlike you and your fool of an uncle, I chose to serve those greater than ourselves, rather than vainly battle with them."

"You sold us out!" I shout. Then confusion kicks in. "But . . . I don't understand. In Slawter, when we were trying to escape from the demons, you helped us."

"No," she smiles. "That was all a pretense. When I first visited your house with Davida Haym, I used magic to convince Dervish to come to Slawter and bring you and Billy with him. On the set it was my job to win your confidence. I found out your secrets, so we could use them against you.

"I played you like pawns," she boasts. "I had you thinking I was one of your pathetic group, a trusted ally. I let you make escape plans and even allowed you to act on them — it would have been more delicious if you failed with freedom in sight. At the end, just before you breached the barrier, I meant to reveal my true self and turn you over to my master. And I would have, except . . ."

"You were knocked unconscious." I gasp, remembering the dying demon who clubbed her in its death throes.

Juni nods bitterly. "By the time I recovered, it was too late. I paused to silence Chuda Sool — he knew the truth about me — then departed to join my master and plot our next approach."

"We had not planned to strike so soon," Lord Loss says. He's come to a stop ten feet away, enjoying my growing understanding of how we were betrayed. "I could sense the magic within you, even though you hid it masterfully. I didn't want to move on you until I knew precisely what I'd have to deal with. But then Juni had a vision."

"I catch glimpses of the future," Juni says smugly. "I saw you change into a werewolf a few months before it happened."

"I could not wait any longer," Lord Loss sighs. "I wished to punish you while you were human — there would be no satisfaction in killing a senseless animal. So I set a watch on you. I'm a fine judge of werewolves. I was confident of timing it so that I struck just prior to the final turning — I liked the idea of letting you suffer the agonies of the impending change for as long as possible."

"It all fell neatly into place in the end," Juni smirks. "I was planning to come to Carcery Vale, looking for an excuse to explain my return. When your friend died, I donned my psychologist's disguise, disposed of William Mauch, and replaced him. You and Billy couldn't have been more welcoming. And Dervish . . . Well, *he* was positively overjoyed to see me."

"You betrayed us," I snarl, blinking away angry tears.

"You were easy to betray," she murmurs. I can see the wickedness in her eyes. How did I ever miss it? "Dervish fell for my pretty pink eyes and cool white skin. He never looked into my heart. I didn't even have to use magic on him — he fell in love with me of his own accord. The sap."

I feel magic flare within me when she says that. Howling, I bring my fists up. Energy shoots from my knuckles, a ball of pure, invisible power. I direct it at Juni, meaning to blast her into a million fleshy pieces.

Alarm ripples across her eyes. She starts to cast a protective spell but it's too late. I'm going to destroy her, rip her atoms apart, and . . .

Lord Loss sticks out four of his arms. He blocks Juni from the force of my blow and absorbs the energy. Flinches, staggers back a few yards, then rights himself and smiles.

"You are powerful, Grubitsch, but untrained. Perhaps if you had spent more time learning the ways of magic you would be able to control that great force and defend yourself and these other unfortunate victims. But you ran from your responsibility. Therefore you — and all around you — will die."

I scream at him, then unleash a second blast of magic energy, more powerful than the first. It strikes him in the middle of his chest, drives him back several more yards. He knocks Juni to the floor and almost loses his balance. But then he straightens and laughs. Brushes away drops of blood as if cleaning fluff from a jacket.

"Have you finished, or do you want to try again?" he asks. "Maybe you will be luckier the third time. What do you think, Miss Swan?"

Juni's getting back to her feet, irate at having been knocked down. "I think we should take him now and drop the games," she snaps.

"'Take me'?" I repeat. "Take me where?"

"My realm," Lord Loss says. "You surely didn't think I'd kill you here, along with these meaningless others, quickly and cleanly? Dear me, no. You robbed me of my great joy in life — chess. You must pay properly for that, in the universe of the Demonata, where time passes oh, so slowly, where I can torture your soul for a thousand years . . . maybe more."

"A bit harsher than detention after school, wouldn't you say?" Juni sneers.

"Artery," Lord Loss calls. The child-shaped demon with fire instead of eyes pulls his head out of the flight attendant's stomach cavity and looks up, guts dribbling down his chin.

"Spine," Lord Loss says. The giant scorpion sheathes its stinger and regards its master from the ceiling, where it's hanging upside down.

"Femur," Lord Loss finishes, and the rabbitlike demon hops onto the head of a corpse, acid frothing from its lips.

Lord Loss points beyond me to where the majority of the survivors are huddled, terrified and weeping. "Make quick work of them. We must leave soon, before our window home closes."

The familiars laugh horrifically, then race toward me. I flinch as the monstrous creatures draw close to me, but they veer around and leave me untouched. Screams behind — then awful ripping, munching, stabbing, sizzling sounds.

I don't look back. Part of me wants to. Maybe my magic would work against the familiars. Perhaps I could kill them. But I dare not turn my back on Lord Loss. The demon master is the greatest threat. If I let him attack me from behind, I'm definitely doomed.

Hell, who am I trying to kid? I'm doomed anyway. He's shown that he can take my worst and shrug it off. I might as well surrender and get it over and done with. And if he promised me a quick death, maybe I'd take that way out. But I don't like the sound of a millennium of torture in his webbed, wicked world. I'm not going to willingly sacrifice myself to such a miserable fate. If he wants to turn me into one of his long-term playthings, he'll have to fight for me.

"Come on then, you lumpy, ugly amateur!" I yell, backing away from him. "You think you can take me? You're wrong. You'll fail, just like you failed to beat me at chess and kill me in Slawter. You're pathetic!"

Lord Loss's face twists. His arms extend toward me. Power crackles in the air as fierce magic gathers in his misshapen fingertips. I bid farewell to life and steel myself to die.

Then his expression mellows and his arms drop. "No, Grubitsch." He chuckles. "I won't be provoked. You hope to goad me into killing you swiftly. A clever ploy, but I shall not fall for your trick. I came to take you, and take you I will. I'll kill you later, when we are . . ."

A burst of heat to my left makes him pause. It's coming from the wall of the cabin. I glance at it, expecting another of Lord Loss's familiars to appear. The wall's glowing with a white-hot magical light.

"Master?" Juni says uncertainly as Lord Loss draws to a halt.

"Quiet," he snaps.

They don't know what it is!

I move closer to the light, ignoring the heat, figuring if this is something Lord Loss isn't controlling, it can only be good news. Maybe the plane is coming apart and this is the start of a giant explosion. If so, I want to be caught square in the blast. That would wipe the smirk from the demon master's wretched mug.

An oval hole appears in the side of the plane. About six feet from bottom to top and three feet wide. I see a man through the hole, outside, clinging to the wing of the plane. It's the bum! He's been following me for the past few weeks, waiting to see if I turn into a werewolf. He was lurking near my house last night when I burst free of the cellar where Dervish had me caged. I thought he was one of the Lambs — werewolf executioners par excellence — but now I'm starting to have doubts.

The bum half leans into the cabin and stretches out a hand to me, holding on to the wing of the plane with his other hand as a fierce, unearthly wind whips at his hair and clothes. "Boy!" he shouts. "Come with me. *Now!*"

"No!" Lord Loss and Juni scream at the same moment.

Lord Loss's arms snap up and he unleashes a magical shot of energy at the bum. But the white light around the edges of the hole absorbs the power and disperses it in a shower of crackling sparks.

I'm staring stupidly at the tramp, jaw slack, mind in a spin.

"Boy!" the bum shouts again. "I can't take another blast like that. Come now or die."

I look from him to Lord Loss and Juni. Their faces are filled with hate. Juni's muttering a spell, lips moving incredibly fast. Lord Loss is readying himself for a second shot at the bum.

A quick look in the other direction. Artery, Spine, and Femur are rushing up the aisle, desperate to pin me down.

I face Lord Loss again, grin, and flip him the finger. Then I dive toward the bum, sticking out my right hand. The man grabs it and hurls me through the hole. He shouts a word of magic and the hull of the plane starts to close. I hear Lord Loss bellow with fury. Then the hole seals itself and there's only the roaring howl of the wind.

I realize I'm clinging to a bum on the wing of an airplane, thousands of feet above the face of the earth. I have a split second to marvel at the craziness of that. Then the wind grabs us. We're ripped loose. The plane soars onward.

We fall.

# FLIGHT

✠ ✠ ✠

DROPPING at a stomach-punching speed toward the earth. Freefall. Surrounded by blue sky, clouds far below but getting closer every second. I glance desperately at the bum, praying to spot the hump of a parachute pack. But there's nothing. He's falling the same way I am, with only one way of stopping — the *hard* way.

I scream and flap frantically with my arms. Crazily, I wish I was back in the plane. At least I stood a glimmer of a chance with the demons. This is death for certain.

"Boy!" the bum shouts cheerfully. "Are you having fun?"

"We're going to die!" I roar, clothes rippling madly on my limbs, the scream of the wind ice-cold in my ears.

"Not today," the bum chortles, then angles his body and glides closer toward me. "We can fly."

"You're a lunatic!" I shriek.

"Perhaps," he grins, then arcs his body up, pulls away from me, swoops over and beneath me, and draws up on the other side. "Or maybe not."

"Let me hold on to you!" I yell, grabbing for him.

He pulls away. "No. It's time you learned to fend for your-self. You're a creature of magic. Use your power."

"I can't," I howl.

"Of course you can." He tuts as if he's a teacher and we're debating an argument in class, safe on the ground, instead of hurtling toward it at a speed I don't even want to think about.

"We're going to die," I shout again.

"I'm not," he says. "You won't either if you focus. But you'd better be quick," he adds as we enter a thick bank of clouds, then burst through it a second or two later. "You don't have much time." He points at the earth, which I can see clearly now that we've broken through the clouds.

I start to scream senselessly, thoughts wild, gravity pulling me to my high-impact doom. Then the bum asks casually, "Are you cold?"

The craziness of the question draws a furious response. "What sort of a nut are you? I'm falling to my death and you're discussing the temperature!"

"Answer me," he says calmly. "Are you cold?"

"No. But what the —"

"At this height, don't you think you should be? It was in the region of minus forty Fahrenheit on the wing of the air-plane. Any normal person would have felt the icy bite imme-diately. You didn't because magic kept you warm. It can also keep you aloft — *if* you direct it."

"What do I have to do?" I moan, the landscape filling my vision, surely no more than half a minute away from a bone-crunching collision.

"Visualize a bird," the bum says. "Think of the way it flies, how it soars out of a dive with the slightest tilt of its wings. Don't picture your arms as wings or anything like that. Just imagine a bird and fix it in your thoughts."

I do as he says. Close my eyes and think of a swallow swooping and soaring. I've seen them fly many times, when walking home from school or looking out of my bedroom window, glimpsed through the uppermost branches of the forest. They make it look simple — nudge out a wing, duck or pull up their head, catch the wind currents, sail them as if it was the most natural thing in the world.

My head rises. The roar of the wind lessens. A new sensation. Not one of falling, but of . . .

I open my eyes. I'm moving away from the earth, arms by my side, legs straight, head facing the clouds, the bum by my side. *Flying.*

"There," the bum says with a wicked little grin. "Simple, aye?"

Flying high. A creature of the sky. Laughing and hollering with delight. Flying on my front, back, sides — however I please. Somersaulting midair, a far greater rush than any roller-coaster.

"This is amazing!" I yell at the bum, who flies nearby. "How am I doing it?"

"Magic," he says.

"But I'm not trying. I'm not casting spells."

"True magicians don't need spells most of the time."

I stare at him, stunned. "But I'm not a magician."

"No?" He nods at the earth far below. "Then how do you explain this?"

"But Dervish said . . . I've never . . . Bartholomew Garadex!" I throw the name out desperately.

"You're different from Bartholomew," the bum says. "Different from every magician I've ever known or heard about. But you're a magician nonetheless. You draw your power directly from the universe, like the Demonata."

Mention of the demons reminds me of the plane and its doomed passengers. "We have to go back!" I shout, cursing myself for flying around happy and carefree while Lord Loss and his familiars wreak havoc. "We have to save the people on the plane."

The bum sighs. "Dead, all of them."

"No! They can't be! We have to —"

"They're dead," the bum says stiffly. "And even if they aren't, what could we do?"

"Fight!" I roar.

"Against Lord Loss?" He shakes his head. "I'm powerful, boy, and so are you, but Lord Loss is a demon master. We wouldn't last long in a battle with him."

"We have to try," I whisper, thinking of all those men, women, and children. Picturing the Demonata and Juni Swan at savage work. "If we abandon them . . ."

"We've already abandoned them," the bum grunts. "The choice was made when I pulled you out. Everyone on that airplane is dead, and it has crashed — or will shortly — destroying the evidence."

"You let them die." I gasp.

The bum shrugs. "I would have saved them if I could. I've devoted my life to protecting humanity from the Demonata. But some battles you can't win. Some you can't even fight."

Flying in silence. Thinking about what happened and what the bum said. Cold inside, and scared. Unable to get the faces of the people — *the dead* — out of my mind. Yet a big part of me is secretly glad we didn't go back, that the bum spared me another run-in with the demons.

"This is insane," I mutter, looking at the world beneath. "Who are you? What were you doing on the plane? Why have you been following me? I thought you were one of the Lambs. I know nothing about you. I need —"

"Soon," the bum hushes me. "I'll answer all your questions once we're safe on the ground. For now, just fly."

And since there's no point arguing, I tuck my arms in tighter, pick up speed, trail the bum through the air and try — unsuccessfully — to push the faces of the dead from my thoughts.

✠ We fly for hours, mostly above the clouds where people on the ground can't see us. I spot the occasional plane but the bum always steers us clear. A shame — I love the thought of gliding up to one and tapping on the windows, scaring the living daylights out of the passengers and crew.

I've no idea where we are. I didn't ask Juni where we were going when we set off, and I don't know how long I was asleep, so I can't judge how far from home we might have been when the demons attacked.

*Juni . . .*

Rage seethes inside me every time I think about her. I trusted her. I thought she was on my side, that she loved me like a mother. And all the time she was playing me for a fool, setting me up for Lord Loss, cutting me off from Dervish.

I want to quiz the bum about her. Find out where she comes from, how she operates, where I can find her — so I can track her down and burn her for the evil witch she is. But this isn't the right time. I have loads of questions for the tramp. So much I want to know, that I need to find out. Hell, I haven't even asked his name yet!

✠ Finally, five or six hours after I bailed out of the plane, the bum guides me down. The land is barren desert, more rocky than sandy. No signs of human life — it's been the better part of an hour since I saw any kind of house.

"This is the complicated part," the bum says as we come in to land. "The easiest way is to hover a bit above the ground, then stop thinking about birds. After a few seconds you'll fall."

"Can't we touch down?" I ask.

"I can, but I've had a lot of practice. If you try it, you'll probably hit hard and break a leg or arm."

He spreads his arms and drifts down, landing lightly on his feet. I'm tempted to copy him, to prove I'm nimbler than he gives me credit for. But it's been a *long* day and the last thing I want is to break any bones. So I float to within a few feet of the rocky soil, then empty my head of images of birds. For a couple of seconds nothing happens. Then I drop suddenly, stomach lurching.

I hit the ground awkwardly, landing face-first in the dust.

Sitting up, I splutter and wipe dirt and grit from my cheeks, then get to my feet and look around. We're in the middle of nowhere. Some rocky outcrops and hills, a few rustling cacti, nothing else. "Where are we?"

"Home," the bum says, and starts walking toward one of the hills.

"Whose home?" I ask, hurrying after him.

"Mine."

"And you are . . . ?"

He stops and looks back, surprised. "You don't know?"

"Should I?"

"Surely Dervish told . . ." He trails off into silence, then laughs. "All that time in the air, you didn't know whom you were with?"

"I was going to ask but it didn't seem like the right moment," I huff.

The bum shakes his head. "I'm Beranabus." The name sounds familiar but I can't place it.

"Beranabus what?" I ask.

"Just Beranabus," he says, then starts walking again. "Come. We have much to discuss but it will hold. I never feel safe in the open."

With a nervous glance around, I hasten after the shabbily dressed man. Several minutes later we come to the mouth of a cave. Not having had the best experience with caves recently, I pause and peer suspiciously into the shadows.

"It's fine," Beranabus assures me. "This is a safe place, protected by its natural position and the strongest spells I could muster. You have nothing to fear."

"Easy for you to say," I grunt, unconvinced.

Beranabus smiles. He has crooked, stained teeth. This close I can see that his small eyes are grey and his skin is pale beneath a covering of grime and dirt. He's wearing an old, dusty suit. The only fresh thing about him is a small bunch of flowers jutting out of one of his buttonholes.

"If I wanted to harm you," he says, "I could have done so already, with far less effort than it would take on the ground. That should be self-evident."

"I know," I mutter. "It's just . . . I don't like caves."

"With good reason," he says understandingly. "But this isn't like the cave in Carcery Vale. You'll be safe here. I promise."

I hesitate a moment longer, then shrug. "What the hell," I grunt, and push ahead of Beranabus, acting like I couldn't care less.

The cave only runs back fifteen feet or so, then stops. I look for a way out, studying the walls and floor, but I can't see any. "Are you like a monk who doesn't believe in material possessions?" I ask.

"No," Beranabus says, squeezing past me. He touches the ground and mutters a few words of magic. A hole appears. There's a rope ladder attached to the wall at one side, leading down into the dark.

I move to the edge of the hole and look down nervously. There are torches set in the walls, so it's not as dark as it seemed at first. But it runs a long way down and I can only vaguely see the bottom.

"I thought you said a magician didn't need to cast spells," I say, delaying the moment when I have to descend.

"*Most* of the time," Beranabus reminds me. "There are occasions when even the strongest of us must focus our magical energy with words." He sits and swings his legs into the hole. Turns, grabs the ladder, and starts down. Looks up at me before his head bobs beneath my feet. "This will close in a few minutes. If you're coming, get a move on."

"Just waiting for you to get out of my way," I retort. Then, when his head's clear, I ignore the butterflies in my stomach, sit, turn, and climb down the swaying ladder after him.

The hole closes with a small grinding noise before I hit the ground. I try not to think about the fact that I'm shut off from the world. At the base I step clear of the ladder and find myself in a large, bright cave. There are chairs, a sofa, a long table at one end with a vase of flowers on it, a few statues, books, chests of drawers, other bits and pieces. There's also a fire in the middle of the cave, by which a bald, dark-skinned boy sits warming his hands.

"I'm back," Beranabus calls.

"I noticed," the boy replies without looking around.

"I've brought a guest."

The boy's head turns a fraction. He has bright blue eyes and a sour expression. "I thought you were going to kill him."

I stiffen as Beranabus scowls. "I said I *might* have to kill him."

"What do you —," I start to ask angrily.

"Later," Beranabus soothes me, then points to a blanket-spread out on the ground close to the wall. "Get some sleep. I will too. Later we can have a long discussion over a hot meal."

"You think I can sleep after all that's happened?" I snort.

"I know you can," Beranabus says. "Magic. All you have to do is imagine it and you'll sleep like a baby."

"What if I don't want to?"

"You're exhausted. You need rest so you can focus on our conversation and ask all the questions I'm sure are welling up inside you. You wouldn't be able to process my answers in your current state."

I don't want to sleep — I want to tear straight into the explanations — but what he says makes sense. Just keeping my eyelids open is a major effort at the moment.

"One thing first," I mutter. "Dervish and Bill-E — are they OK?"

Beranabus shrugs. "I think so."

"You're not sure?"

"No. But Lord Loss and *Juni*" — for some reason he sneers as he says her name — "don't know where we went once we left the plane. I doubt Juni would risk going back in case we got there before her."

"You'll warn Dervish?" I ask. "About Juni working with Lord Loss?"

"I can't contact him immediately," Beranabus says, "but I'll get word to him as soon as I can. He'll have to fend for himself until then."

That's not satisfactory but it's the best he's going to offer. So, since I'm worn out and there's nothing I could do even if I were in my best shape, I stumble to the blanket and lie down fully clothed. I doubt I can fall asleep as easily as Beranabus expects, but as soon as I close my eyes and think about it, I find myself going under. Seconds later I'm comatose.

# POWER OF THE BEAST

�҂ ✚ ✚

A LOAF of fresh bread is waved underneath my nose. I come out of sleep smiling, the scent of warm goodness filling my nostrils. For a few groggy moments I think I'm at home with Dervish, it's a Sunday morning, no school, no worries, a long, lazy day stretching deliciously ahead of me.

Then my eyes focus. I see the lined fingers clutching the bread and the bearded face beyond. I remember. And all the good thoughts disappear in an instant.

"How long was I asleep?" I yawn, sitting up, wincing from the pain in my back — I'm not used to sleeping on a stone floor.

"Many hours," Beranabus says, handing me the bread.

"Eight? Ten? Twelve?"

He shrugs.

I look for my watch but the strap must have snapped during the night of my turning. Standing, I rub the sides of my back, stretch, and groan. "Haven't you heard of beds?" I complain.

"You'll grow accustomed to the floor after a few months."

I squint at him. *Months?* I have no intention of being here that long. But before I can challenge him, he walks over to the fire where the sour-faced boy is still perched close to the flames. I follow, tearing a chunk out of the loaf, gobbling it. The bread's chewy and I don't have any butter, but I'm so hungry I could happily eat cardboard.

Beranabus sits close to the boy. I stay on my feet, studying the curious couple. Ancient Beranabus and the teenager, not much older than me. The shabby, bearded, hairy, suited magician and the boy — his apprentice or servant? — in drab but clean clothes, completely bald. The boy's dark flesh is laced with small scars and fading bruises. The tips of the two smallest fingers on his left hand are missing. His eyes have a faraway, miserable look. He wears no shoes. Beranabus is barefoot too, his boots discarded.

"Grubitsch Grady, meet Kernel Fleck," Beranabus introduces us.

"Grubbs," I correct him, sticking out a hand. The boy only grunts. "What about your name?" I ask, trying to be friendly despite his cold welcome. "Is it Colonel, like in the army?"

"No. Kernel, like in popcorn," Beranabus answers after a few seconds of stony silence. "It's short for something longer, but neither of us can remember what."

Kernel sniffs and faces the fire. There are sausages speared on a stick close by. He picks up the stick and jams the sausages into the flames. Mutters a spell. The heat of the fire increases and the sausages cook in seconds. He takes one off, blows on it, and eats it, then takes off another and gives it to Beranabus. After a pause, he removes a third sausage and offers it to me.

"Thanks," I say, biting into it. Too hot, but delicious. I ravenously munch my way through it, then gratefully accept another.

"Kernel does most of the cooking," Beranabus says, holding a sausage in one hand, picking at dirt beneath the nails of his right foot with the other.

"I have to," Kernel says. "He'd eat the food raw if I didn't."

"It's all the same once your stomach processes it," Beranabus snorts. "Hot, cold, cooked, raw . . . it doesn't make any difference when you're squatting over a hole."

"A hole?" I frown.

"No toilets," Kernel says, looking at Beranabus sourly.

Kernel cooks some chicken legs, again using his spell. (I wonder where they get the food from, but don't ask.) He piles them on a dusty, cracked plate, then cooks some ribs and potatoes. That done, he takes what he wants from the plate and passes it across.

Beranabus bites into his chicken leg, then looks over at me. "Tell me everything about the past few months. I know a lot already, but I want the complete story. When you realized your body was changing, how the magic developed, the way you dealt with it."

"I thought *you* were the one who was going to provide answers."

"I will," he promises. "But you first. It will make my job easier."

While we eat, I fill him in on all that has happened, discovering my magical ability after Slawter, fighting it, the sickness, using magic to counter the threat of the werewolf.

"Why did you fight the magic in the first place?" he interrupts. "Most people would be thrilled if they found themselves in your position."

"I know what magic entails," I say quietly. "It's linked to the Demonata. I've been part of that crazy universe before. I didn't want to get sucked into it again."

Beranabus and Kernel share a look. Then Beranabus tells me to continue.

I explain about the cave we unearthed in Carcery Vale, going there under the influence of the beast, digging through the rubble blocking the entrance, Loch's accident, Dervish covering up, Juni entering our lives.

"Who's Juni Swan?" Kernel asks Beranabus.

"One of Lord Loss's assistants," Beranabus says, squinting. "Actually, she . . ." He stops and clears his throat. "We can discuss Miss Swan and her background later. Finish, please, Grubitsch."

"It's Grubbs," I correct him again, then cover the past couple of days and nights, the werewolf taking over, killing Billy's grandparents, Juni whipping me out of town and betraying me on the plane. I tell the story as quickly as I can, eager to get it out of the way. I don't go into all the details, like the voice and the face in the rock, figuring they're not important. I can tell Beranabus about them later.

Beranabus listens silently, then spends a couple of minutes thinking about what I've said. "The boy who fell," he finally says, echoing Dervish's concerns when he first came to the cave. "Was it definitely an accident? Nobody else was —"

"No," I cut in. "We were alone, just the three of us. He slipped, fell, died. An accident. No demons or evil mages were involved."

"Good," Beranabus grunts. "When I heard the entrance had been excavated and someone had died in the cave, I feared the worst — especially since my spells of warning hadn't worked. I should have been alerted the moment the first rock was lifted out. I assumed a powerful mage had spun a counterspell and was preparing the way for a demon invasion. I've never moved so quickly in my life."

"He ran like his feet were on fire," Kernel says, smiling for the first time — but it's a brief, thin smile.

"Dervish told me about the cave," I say softly. "How it was used as a crossing point for demons. He said the tunnel between universes could be reopened, that the Demonata could come through in their thousands and take over our world. You don't think Juni and Lord Loss . . . ?"

"No." Beranabus smiles wryly, showing his crooked, discolored teeth. "Lord Loss has no interest in opening tunnels between universes. Most demons want to destroy humanity, but Lord Loss thrives on human misery. He's as keen to keep that tunnel closed as we are."

Beranabus picks at his teeth with a thin chicken bone. His breath stinks. In fact, most of him stinks. He obviously isn't concerned about personal hygiene. Finally, laying the bone aside, he speaks again. "The cave brought me to Carcery Vale, but you're why I stayed. I could feel the power in you, bursting to be released. I wanted to be there when it exploded — or when you imploded."

"*Imploded?*"

"You could have burned up. If the magic hadn't found an outlet, it would have destroyed you from within. There was no way of telling until the full moon, when I knew you'd be pushed to the point where you and the beast had to settle the matter once and for all.

"The werewolf is the key," he continues. "The curse of the Gradys. Many centuries ago, your ancestors bred with demons."

"*Bred?*" I yelp. "No way!"

"It doesn't happen often," Beranabus says. "Most demons are physically incompatible with humans. But it's not unheard of. When such unions occur, the offspring are never natural. Humans and demons weren't meant to mix. When they do, their children are freaks of the highest order, neither human nor demon, caught painfully between. Most die at birth. But some survive."

His face is dark, shadows flickering across it from the flames of the fire. "A few grow and thrive, either in the demon's universe or ours. Your ancestor's child was one of those. The magical strand of the Demonata stayed hidden, at least long enough for the child to mature and bear children of its own. When its demonic legacy finally surfaced, the victim turned into a wolflike creature."

"So the Demonata are to blame," I growl, hating them afresh. "I gathered as much from Dervish, but I was never sure."

"I don't know about *blame,*" Beranabus says. "Such couplings are often set in motion by humans. Your ancestor quite possibly made the first approach, and . . ." He twirls his fingers suggestively.

"Here comes the bride," mutters Kernel.

Beranabus looks into the flames, considering his next words. "You're a unique specimen, even for a Grady. I've never seen or heard of anyone like you. Magic is unpredictable, chaotic. It works differently in each person. But there are general rules that have always applied — until now. You shattered all of them."

"Is that a good or a bad thing?" I ask.

"I don't know. It's the reason I didn't approach you immediately. I wasn't sure how you'd change, what the magic would do when it surfaced. Of course there was Juni to consider too. I didn't know how close you and Dervish were to her, if you knew whom she served."

"Of course we didn't!" I bellow. "Lord Loss killed my parents and sister. Do you think —"

"Peace," Beranabus says. "I trust you now, but I couldn't before. For all I knew, you and Dervish were in league with Juni Swan, and I was being lured into a trap. Dervish himself might have opened the entrance to the cave to entice me to Carcery Vale."

"Have you been paranoid for long?" I ask cynically.

"I learned a long time ago not to trust anybody," he replies tightly. "Not until they've proved themselves worthy. And even then I keep a close watch on them."

"I've been with Beranabus for thirty years or more," Kernel says, "and I still wake up sometimes to find him giving me the evil eye."

"Thirty years?" I study the boy again. "You can't be that old."

"We'll come to that soon," Beranabus says before Kernel can respond. "Let's finish with your magic first. Where was I?"

"You were waxing poetic about how unique he was," Kernel reminds him.

"Aye." Beranabus's face lights up. "In every other magician, the gift of magic is evident from birth. Even if they're unaware of their potential, other magicians can sense it. Dervish should have seen the magic within you but he didn't. Because you hid it from him. From yourself too."

"No. I knew it was there."

"You knew after Slawter," Beranabus corrects me, "but it didn't start then. This power has been with you since you were born. Some secret part of you knew what you were from the day you came into this world — but it was afraid. It didn't want the power and responsibility. So it pushed the magic down deep where it couldn't work or even be noticed.

"No other magician can do that. They can deny their calling and refuse to hone their talent, but they can't bury it completely. But you were so powerful that even as a child you were instinctively able to hide your magic from the world. If not for the Grady curse, it would have lain hidden for the rest of your life, a great power wasted."

"I wish it had," I mutter angrily.

"You shouldn't," scolds Beranabus. "If not for the magic, you'd be a wild, raging animal now. The barriers you erected between yourself and your magical potential began to crumble when you first faced demons. You had to draw on your inner power when you fought Lord Loss and his familiars. You drove your magic back down afterward, but cracks had appeared in your armor.

"The magic has been buzzing around inside you ever since, trying to break free. You kept a lid on it for a long time, but then the curse kicked in. The werewolf came to the forefront. That should have been the end of Grubitsch Grady. But the magician within you opposed the beast. You said you used magic to fight the change, but you're wrong — magic used you. It stopped you from becoming a monster."

"No, it didn't," I say guiltily. "I turned for a while. I killed Ma and Pa Spleen. Next time, when the moon's full and the werewolf takes over, I'll kill again."

"Do you really believe that?" Beranabus asks.

"Of course." I stare at him, confused.

He shakes his head. "The moon has exerted as powerful an influence over you as it ever will. The beast dominated for a short time, but you drove it back. It will rise again, but you'll beat it then too. It will be easier next time. The beast will always be within you, snarling and spitting, battling to break free when the moon sings to it. But you're in control. You won."

"I didn't win!" I snap. "I killed Bill-E's grandparents. That's not winning. Even if I never lose control again, I've already killed. How can you say everything's OK? Maybe you don't count the murder of your half brother's grandparents as a big deal, but I do. So don't —"

"Show him how to remember," Kernel interrupts. "I'm not going to listen to him rant and rave for hours. Teach him the spell — let him see how it really played out. That will shut him up."

"What are you talking about?" I growl.

"A spell to help you recall everything that happened while you were transformed," Beranabus says.

"Why would I want to do that?"

"To learn the truth."

"But I already —"

"Just let him teach you the damn spell," Kernel snaps.

I feel uneasy — I don't want to relive the murders — but they've aroused my curiosity, so I play along. Beranabus tells me to close my eyes and focus on my breathing. I breathe in . . . hold it for five seconds . . . then breathe out. When I have the right rhythm, he tells me the words to use. Breaks them down into simple syllables so I can repeat them, even though I don't know what they mean.

As I draw toward the end of the spell, a screen forms within my thoughts. It's the huge TV screen from home. Blank, grey, like it's on standby. I'm about to tell Beranabus there's no signal, but then the screen flickers. Bursts of light. Static. Then . . .

The cave. Just after I froze the waterfall into ice. I see everything through the eyes of the beast. I'm crouched low, howling, squinting into the light of Juni's flashlight as she pads hesitantly toward me. It's crazy, but as I'm watching, in spite of all I know about her now, I feel concern for Juni. I want her to flee before the wolf attacks. I almost call a warning to her, but then I remember this is a screened replay, it's not happening live.

In the cave, Juni comes within touching distance and regards me coolly. "The great Grubbs Grady changes at last," she sneers, then spits at me. "You pathetic creature! If you knew how much I've loathed these past weeks, having to be nice to you and your mongrel of an uncle."

The beast roars at her and raises its fists to beat her to a pulp. This time I root for the werewolf, wanting it to kill the deceitful witch. But before it can strike, Juni utters a quick spell and it falls to the ground and rolls around with muffled grunts and yelps, before coming to a quivering halt.

"There," Juni smiles, faking nice. "That should hold you."

She puts her flashlight down and walks around me, checking from all angles, then produces a large knife — one from our kitchen! — and lays it by my head. The beast tries to howl but can't. Juni strolls to the wall of the cave, where the crack I created runs up near the icy waterfall. She stares at the ice, then at me, troubled. Shakes her head and chants a spell. I listen for a few minutes.

When the spell shows no sign of ending, I say without opening my eyes, "Is there a fast-forward button on this thing?"

"What's happening?" Beranabus asks.

"I'm in the cave. I've turned. Juni's crafting some long-winded spell."

"Probably calling Lord Loss," Beranabus notes. "Very well. Try this."

He teaches me some new words. Once I've repeated them, the picture fades out, then, after some static and crackling, tunes back in. Juni's still chanting, but she's standing over me now. No sign of Lord Loss, but the wall is red and yellow around the crack and the ice is melting, becoming a normal waterfall again. The heat in the cave is vicious. The beast I've become is sweating.

Juni's holding up the knife. She bends, presses it to the left side of my throat, makes a quick swipe. Blood spurts, drenching the blade. I go stiff, both as the werewolf in the past and me in the present. But then Juni puts her face to the cut, breathes on it, and the wound closes. She moves the blade to the other side of my throat and does the same thing. Then she takes the red blade to the crack in the wall.

"What's happening?" Beranabus asks, and I describe the scene to him. "Strange. I never heard of a demon being summoned that way. But Lord Loss is unique. Nobody knows why he's the only demon master who can cross to our world, or how he does it. This must be a method he taught her."

Juni smears my blood down one side of the rock within the crack, then the other. She steps back and chants more spells, louder, arms thrown wide. Finishes with a triumphant yowl, then leaps away from the crack, covering her eyes.

Nothing happens.

Juni lowers her arm and stares at the crack for a long time, then at the blade, then me. She walks across slowly and looks down, confused.

"Juni . . ." The word comes from deep within the rock. I place the voice right away — Lord Loss. "Juni . . ." he calls again, distant, hungry, anxious.

Juni returns to the crack and talks quickly, softly. I can't hear what she says. But then Lord Loss hisses a name that chills me to the bone. *"Billy Spleen . . ."*

Juni bows, sets the knife down, looks at me, and grins nastily. "Stay where you are, beastie. I'll be back for you soon."

She leaves, not bothering to take the flashlight.

On the floor the werewolf struggles to tear free of its magical constraints. After a while the beast becomes still. Its hands start to glow. The glow spreads and sweeps up its arms, hits its face and chest, then radiates down its body and legs.

The werewolf stands and cocks its head as if listening to someone speak. Then, with a noise that sounds like a growl of agreement, it races for the exit and heads for the surface.

As the beast lurches through the forest, I fill Beranabus and Kernel in on what's happening. Beranabus is unsure what to make of Juni's behavior. "She seems to have been trying to summon Lord Loss. For some reason the spell didn't work. But I don't see what difference the other boy's blood would make."

"I don't think she wanted Bill-E for the spell," I murmur. "And I don't think it failed. Lord Loss stopped her. He wanted Bill-E to be there when he crossed, so he could kill us both."

"Perhaps," Beranabus says, but he doesn't sound convinced.

The chase concludes. The beast arrives at Bill-E's house. The back door is open. The wolf bolts inside and finds Juni picking up the unconscious Bill-E Spleen. Ma and Pa Spleen are both dead. The werewolf howls at Juni. She drops Bill-E as the beast leaps. They fight, my transformed self ripping at the albino with its teeth and claws, Juni fighting back physically, no time for spells. She screams my name and the beast roars. Juni screams my name again and again, each time adding more distress to the cry.

Finally, after a minute of Juni screaming, the werewolf releases her. She staggers back, bloody and stunned. The beast growls angrily, standing firmly between Juni and Bill-E, protecting the otherwise defenseless boy. Then the view goes blurry. I sense the creature changing. Juni sighs with relief, then spreads her hands and talks quickly, faking concern. "Grubbs?" she gasps. "Is that you?"

I open my eyes and the screen disappears inside my head. I stare at Beranabus, openmouthed. "I didn't kill them," I whisper. "I tried to save them. I protected Bill-E. *I didn't kill them!*" The last sentence comes out as a sob. I bend over and weep with relief, all else forgotten, eternally grateful to be innocent Grubbs Grady again — not the loathsome killer that I mistakenly believed I was.

# THE VETERAN

✠    ✠    ✠

MY first impulse, when I stop crying, is to rush back to Carcery Vale and warn Dervish and Bill-E of the danger they're in.

"We already had this conversation," Beranabus sighs.

"I don't care," I snap. "Juni didn't just target me — she went after Bill-E too. She might not return to the Vale right away, but she can easily phone Dervish and ask about me. If she discovers he doesn't know where I am or what really happened, she can return and . . ." I shake my head viciously, trying not to think of all the terrible things she could do. "We have to go back and warn them."

"No," Beranabus says softly. "Their welfare isn't my concern."

"How can you say that?" I shriek. "Dervish is your friend."

"No — if anything, he's my employee."

"What do you . . . ?" I stop, finally realizing where I had heard Beranabus's name before. Dervish mentioned it when he was explaining about his work. I should have put two and two together when he was talking about the warning spells at the cave, but my head's still in a whirl. "You're the boss of the Disciples," I mutter.

"I wouldn't describe myself that way," Beranabus sniffs. "I don't have much to do with them. I use the Disciples where appropriate, but I fight most of my battles in the Demonata's universe, alone."

"Not *quite* alone," Kernel huffs.

Beranabus grunts offhandedly at Kernel, then addresses me again. "I didn't form the Disciples. They came to me looking for leadership and training. I occasionally demand their help but have no vested interest in the group."

"But Dervish is one of your people," I argue. "He told me you sent him to Carcery Vale to protect the cave. You're responsible for him."

"No!" Beranabus barks. He brushes his long hair back from his face, glowering at me. "I sent Dervish to Carcery Vale, as I sent others before him, to watch for demons and their human servants, to report to me if any came sniffing in search of the cave. Everything else in his life was secondary to that task. He should have respected my instructions, kept a low profile, and not gotten entangled with a demon master like Lord Loss. He brought this trouble on himself. I don't have time to get involved in personal conflicts. Lord Loss has nothing to do with the cave, so I don't care what he does to Dervish."

"You're a monster," I sneer. "You're no better than the Demonata."

"Perhaps not," Beranabus concedes. "But the Disciples understand that there are forces at work in the universe far more important than anything in their own lives. They accept the need to put human concerns behind them and focus on the nobler cause to which they've been called."

"I don't do noble causes," I retort. "I care about Dervish and Bill-E. That's all. They're more important to me than anything else, even the safety of the bloody world."

"He's arrogant and stupid," Kernel says, staring at me coldly. "He can't see the bigger picture. You made a mistake bringing him here. Send him back. Let him perish at the hands of Lord Loss."

"That isn't your decision to make," Beranabus says, eyes flashing. "Don't forget your place. You're here to serve."

"Well, it's true." Kernel pouts.

Beranabus takes a steadying breath, then faces me again. "What I'm trying to explain," he says, only barely restraining his anger, "is that Dervish wouldn't want us to rush back. He understands the importance of my work and knows I don't get involved in minor skirmishes — which is all this is. He doesn't expect me to ride to his rescue. This quarrel with Lord Loss and Juni Swan is of his own making, and he must deal with them himself.

"Having said that," Beranabus continues, raising his voice to stop me from interrupting, "I *will* get word to him, as I promised. I can't get in touch with him now — there are no easy means of making contact with the outside world from here — but as soon as I can, I'll warn him of Juni's treachery and the threat he faces. That's the best I can offer. And it's all Dervish would expect."

"Fine," I grunt, getting to my feet. "But I'm not one of your Disciples, so I don't have to obey your rules. I'll go and warn him right now if you'll just point me in the right direction . . ." I look at him challengingly, expecting an argument.

Beranabus smiles flatly. "Once you leave the cave, the fastest route is east. It's a long, hard walk. The sun is merciless, water holes are few and far between, and there's little food to be found. An experienced trekker or a magician might make it out alive. But you're not a worldly traveler, and you don't know how to make the most of your magical potential. You'll be dead within a week. If you want to make the attempt regardless, go ahead. I won't detain you."

"Right," I nod sharply. "I will."

I start toward the rope ladder but Kernel stops me. "Grubitsch . . . Grubbs. He's telling the truth. You can't make it. You'll die if you try."

"I'd rather die trying than live and let Dervish and Bill-E be butchered."

"It would be pointless," Kernel argues. "Even if you got out alive, it would take weeks to reach civilization. Dervish will find out quicker through us. Disciples visit here regularly. One might come tomorrow or the next day. You won't achieve anything by sacrificing yourself. Do you want us to tell your uncle you wasted your life on a pointless mission? How do you think that would make him feel?"

I stare at Kernel coldly, then turn slowly to Beranabus. "You swear you'll let him know as soon as you can?"

The magician nods. "As Kernel said, we receive several visitors a year. When the next Disciple comes, I'll give him or her a message to pass on to Dervish."

"What if it's months before anyone visits?"

Beranabus doesn't reply.

I think it over. Weigh the pros and cons. Try to decide what Dervish would tell me to do. I finally figure it makes no sense to leave.

"OK." I sigh, taking my place by the fire. "I don't like it, and I'll hold you responsible if anything happens to Dervish or Bill-E. But I'm going to trust you. I don't know for sure that I should, but to hell with it. Now, I assume you brought me here for a purpose. What is it?"

Beranabus laughs. "Damn it all, I like you! You're blunt and to the point. I'm sure you'll cause me all sorts of aggravation, but I'm looking forward to having you around."

"Never mind the compliments," I growl. "Just tell me why I'm here."

"Very well. As I explained, I don't have much to do with the Disciples. They deal with largely unimportant matters. They stop some demons from crossing and limit the damage caused by those who get through. That doesn't mean much in the universal scheme of things. Hundreds of casualties . . . a few thousand . . . even a few million . . . what of them?"

I gape at the elderly bum, then at Kernel. "Is he for real?"

"You'd better believe it," Kernel says in a low voice, looking at Beranabus darkly.

"I can't waste time worrying about a few dead humans," Beranabus defends himself. "I have more important work to tend to."

"What's more important than saving lives?" I challenge him.

"Saving the world," he answers without the least hint of irony. "Most of the demons who hit our universe are weak. It's relatively easy for a sly demon — with human assistance — to create a window between their universe and ours, but the masters can't squeeze through. Occasionally, a tunnel can be opened — like at the cave in Carcery Vale — that more powerful demons can access. But most of the time only the lesser Demonata can cross, and they can't stay more than a few minutes. A nuisance, aye, but they don't threaten the existence of the human race.

"I focus on combating the threat of the stronger monsters, those who could wipe out mankind. They're always looking for ways to cross. The Disciples act when they uncover evidence on this world of a potential crossing, but I can't allow that to happen with the masters. I have to prevent such threats in their infancy.

"To do that, Kernel and I work in the universe of the Demonata. Unlike the Disciples, we spend little time on this world. We walk among demons, spying on them, uncovering their plans in the formative stages, wrecking them. We divide demons who are working together. Locate and destroy places where tunnels could be built. It's difficult. We have to fight constantly and the battles are savage."

"Savage," Kernel echoes, his voice a whisper.

"It's a horrible undertaking," Beranabus says. "One might even call it a curse. But it has to be done. The Demonata are a constant threat. Those of us with the power to limit them to their own realm don't have the freedom of choice. Kernel and I know that if we don't fight the monsters on their worlds, the demon masters will cross and fight us on ours — and everyone will perish.

"We went to Carcery Vale as soon as I heard the entrance to the cave had been opened. As I already told you, my warning spells should have been activated instantly, but for whatever reason they didn't work. When Dervish sent word, we rushed to the scene. I feared the handiwork of the Demonata and thought I might be too late to stop them. To my relief I found no evidence of their presence."

"What about Lord Loss?" I cry. "And Juni?"

"They didn't bother me. Lord Loss doesn't want to open a tunnel. He prefers things the way they are. I considered talking with Dervish about Juni, but I didn't know if I could trust him. For all I knew, he'd pledged himself to her dark cause and was working with her to trap me."

"Dervish would never do that," I growl.

"Probably not," Beranabus agrees. "But he might have fallen under her spell. She could have been using him to strike at me. I decided not to reveal my presence. I sent Kernel back here and remained hidden, to ensure no demons came to make use of the cave. I planned to close the entrance again and let Dervish know about Juni before I left. But then I spotted *you*."

The hairs on the back of my neck stand up. I'm no fool. I can see where this is heading. But I say nothing. I act ignorant, hoping I'm wrong, not wanting to put ideas in his head if they aren't already there — though I'm sure they are.

"You'd hidden your magic masterfully," Beranabus says, "but it had started to spill out by the time I arrived. I could see it shining through."

"Dervish and Juni didn't," I mumble. "Juni tested me, searching for magic. She couldn't find any."

"Of course she could," he barks. "You still haven't seen through all of her deceptions. I don't blame you. It's hard, when you've trusted someone, to see them as they really are.

You know Juni was working against you all this time, but you still think of her as a friend.

"Juni's far more powerful than Dervish. She knew the magic was there. Those tests were to check how strong you were, how much of a threat you posed, so she and Lord Loss could plan their assault. I don't think she was able to find out as much about you as she hoped. That's why they decided to confront you in the cave. They chose a place of magic, where Lord Loss would be more powerful. When you escaped, they switched to the airplane, figuring that up in the air you couldn't escape — at worst, they could crash the aircraft and kill you that way.

"Juni's been manipulating you at every step. Worming out your secrets, finding weaknesses to use against you. She's a cunning vixen. She artfully drove a wedge between you and Dervish. Even summoned the Lambs to make you believe he'd sacrificed you to the Grady executioners."

"You mean he didn't?" I gape at Beranabus, ashen-faced.

"Of course not," Beranabus grunts. "You know your uncle. You saw how he fought to save your brother. He would have done the same for you. He's not a man to give up on his loved ones."

I feel cold inside. I thought Dervish had betrayed me, when in fact *I* did the betraying. I should have known he wouldn't call in the Lambs without discussing it first. Dervish always played straight with me, ever since he came to visit me in the asylum and told me that he knew demons were real.

"I've been a fool," I mutter.

"Aye," Beranabus says. "But we all make fools of ourselves one time or another. It's part of being human. But that's beside the point. I was talking about . . ." He frowns and looks to Kernel for help.

"You'd just spotted the shining beacon of magic that was Grubbs Grady," Kernel says dryly, and I realize he's jealous of me.

"Of course. Forgive me, I lose track of my thoughts so easily. Old age and more battles with the Demonata than I care to remember. Yes, I was on the verge of leaving Carcery Vale, satisfied that no demons were lurking in the wings, when *you* caught my eye. I saw your magic, the struggle taking place within you, the power you could wield if you survived. It's not often that I come across such a promising find.

"I stayed to track your development. I staked you out and let you see me from time to time — I hoped your magic would respond to mine. I was trying to load the deck in my favor. I'd apologize, but that would be hypocritical of me."

"Get on with it," I snarl.

"There's not much more to get on with. I spied on Dervish and Juni when I wasn't following you. I knew that witch was up to no good, but I wasn't sure of her exact plans. Then I saw the Lambs arrive. You burst out of the underground cellar. I trailed you to the cave but didn't follow you down — Juni would have sensed my presence. I waited while she came, dealt with you, and left again. Then you burst out of the cave. I pursued you to your brother's house, then the airport. When I realized Juni planned to board an airplane with you, I guessed what her plan was and I followed."

"You could have stopped her," I say icily. "You knew she was going to kill the other passengers. You could have attacked. Ripped me from her before we got on."

"No," he says. "I wasn't sure. She might not have struck on the airplane. Or perhaps she was taking you somewhere else to meet Lord Loss. Maybe you were in league with her. I weighed all my options and I decided to wait. It was the right call, and if I had to make it again I'd do exactly the same thing."

He scowls at the disgusted look I give him, then waves the matter away. "And here we are," he says. "The end of the story."

"Not quite," I reply. "You still haven't said what you want me for, why you rescued me and brought me here."

Beranabus frowns. "Isn't that obvious?"

"Yes. But I want you to say it."

"Very well. You're a magician. I want you to become my assistant, like Kernel, cross into the universe of the Demonata with us, and spend the rest of your life by my side, killing demons."

# THE MONOLITH

✠   ✠   ✠

SITTING on my blanket, legs crossed, hunched over, fingers locked together. Beranabus is at his table, sorting through papers, muttering and whistling. Kernel is exercising, stretching, and limbering up. They're setting off to fight demons shortly. They expect me to go with them.

It's crazy. I told Beranabus I wouldn't do it. Leave my own world? Enter the Demonata's realm? Fight monsters like Lord Loss every day? No bloody way, Jo-bloody-sé!

Beranabus didn't argue. Just shrugged and said we all have to make our own decisions in life, then went to get ready. I sat by the fire a while longer, watching him and Kernel prepare. Then came back here, where I've been sitting for the past half hour, silent, numb.

Kernel finishes stretching. Bends, touches his toes, then rises in the air. Slowly turns a somersault. Lands softly on his feet and lets go of his toes. Spots me watching him and walks over. "Having fun?"

"It's better than a circus." I stare up at him, his scars and bruises, the marks of past battles, the fear in his eyes. "How do you do it?" I whisper. "I've fought demons. I know what it's like. How do you find the courage to . . . ?"

Kernel shrugs like it's no big deal. Licks his lips and glances at Beranabus, then sits beside me. "I never really had a choice," he says. "I had a brother. Well, I thought . . . No, let's leave it at that — it gets too complicated otherwise. He was kidnapped by a demon. I followed after him. Met Beranabus and some others — your uncle was one of them."

"You know Dervish?" I ask, surprised.

"Yes. I haven't seen him in thirty-odd years, but we were good friends back then. I wouldn't have survived without him. Is he still a punk?"

"What?" I frown.

"He was a punk. Spiked hair, earrings, leather jacket, chains."

"No." I chuckle. "We must be talking about a different guy. Dervish was never . . ." I hesitate. How many demon-fighting Disciples called Dervish can there be in the world? "I'll quiz you about that later. Finish telling me about your-self first."

Kernel shrugs. "Things didn't work out with my brother. I returned home, but several years had passed — time works differently in the Demonata's universe. I couldn't pick up the pieces of my old life. I no longer belonged to that world. So I came to work for Beranabus. He taught me how to master my powers and slay demons. I've been doing it ever since."

"What's it like? Do you have days off? Weekends? Holidays?"

Kernel laughs. "Sure — two weeks on a beach of fire in the sunny south of Hades, half price off-season. Of course we don't have holidays! We don't fight *all* the time — we have to rest, and Beranabus occasionally has to do something on this world — but we're at it most days of any given year."

"What do you do when you're not fighting?"

"Recover and relax here."

"You don't get out at all? Not even for a day trip?"

"Day trip to where?" Kernel snorts. "I go up the ladder every now and then for a breath of fresh air. Maybe go for a walk for an hour or two. But it's boiling by day, freezing by night, and there's nothing to see or do."

"Doesn't Beranabus take you with him when he goes away?"

"Rarely," Kernel says hotly. "He prefers it if one of us is here when we're not battling demons, in case anyone tries to contact him. And even when he does take me, it's only ever on business. We're in and out as quickly as possible, keeping a low profile, hiding in the shadows."

He stops. His fingers are trembling. There are hard tears in his eyes, but he's holding them back. I try to think of something comforting to say but can't. I want to change the subject but don't know what to talk to him about. So I ask about his age — not entirely off-topic but hopefully less of a soft spot.

"You said you'd been with Beranabus thirty years, but that can't be right. You don't look more than sixteen or seventeen."

He smiles tiredly. "Like I said, time works differently in the demon universe. It varies from zone to zone. In some places it passes faster than here or at the same rate, but usually it's slower. We're often gone for what feels like a day or two, only to come back to find six months have passed here."

"Bloody hell!" I gasp.

Kernel nods miserably. "In real time I've been with Beranabus for . . . I don't know . . . maybe four or five years. But thirty or more have slipped by on Earth while we've been off fighting demons."

"That's what Beranabus wants me to sign up for?" I gulp. "Spend my life facing demons? Live in a cave when I'm not working? And go out one day to find that decades have passed and everyone I knew is old or dead?"

"It sounds bad when you put it that way." Kernel laughs hollowly. "It has its rewards. I'm more powerful than just about any living human. And I save the planet from unimaginable dangers on a regular basis. But that's not much comfort when I'm rotting away here or being pummeled by a four-headed giant."

Kernel stands and smirks, a hint of pity in his otherwise bitter, mocking smile. "Welcome to the firm." Then he goes to get ready.

✣ Beranabus works on opening a window to the Demonata's universe. It was a big deal for Dervish when he summoned Lord Loss, but Beranabus is more adept. A few spells, some scrawled symbols on the walls, a silly, short dance, and the world starts to fade around us. Smoke pours from Beranabus's flesh, all sorts of shapes, mostly a mix of animals and demons. The roof of the cave becomes momentarily translucent. I spot a red sky full of giant demons streaking across the heavens like meteors. Then the cave firms up again. The smoke clears. And Beranabus is standing in front of a black pillar that is strangely familiar. The word "monolith" pops into my head, but I don't know why.

"Not bad, aye?" Beranabus says. "Kernel is the master of opening windows, but he's at his best in the universe of the Demonata. From here it's as easy for me to do it. But once we cross he's in a league of his own. You'll see what I mean soon enough — if you come with us." He takes a step back from the monolith. "Made up your mind yet?"

"I made it up ages ago," I snap. "I'm not coming."

"Of course you are," Beranabus smiles. "Who could resist a challenge like this? The chance to flex your magical muscles, eliminate scores of demons, save the world. You'll come with us in the end, so why not drop the reluctant act and —"

"I'm not acting!" I shout, flushing angrily. "I've had enough of demons. I don't want to fight them. I don't care how magical I am. I'm not your assistant and I never will be. So just —"

"There are two fields of thought about the granting of magical talent," Beranabus interrupts smoothly. "Some claim it's pure luck, the random lottery of the universe doling out magic without method or purpose. Others — and I'm one of them — believe there's a force that wants humans to triumph. We think magicians are created to keep the world safe from the Demonata, that at times of great peril, heroes are generated, capable of defeating the otherwise unstoppable forces of evil.

"It doesn't matter which is right. You have the power. Whether you gained it by design or accident is irrelevant. You have the ability to kill demons, to stop them crossing. If you don't make the most of that talent — if you hide from your duty — it's because you're a coward, plain and simple."

I tremble with rage at the insult. Part of me wants to call upon all of my newly discovered powers and hit him with the strongest magical blast I can muster, to teach him never to mess with me again. But I don't. Because he's speaking the truth.

Dervish loved me, so he never said it, but he must have thought it. He didn't object when I refused to learn spells and magic. He respected my choice and never made me feel like I was chickening out. I told myself I'd done my bit and now I was entitled to a normal life.

But that was a load of crap. Deep down I knew I didn't want to fight because I was scared. Dervish knew it, I knew it, and now Beranabus knows it. The only difference is, Beranabus has called me on it.

Beranabus is leaning toward me, eyebrows raised, awaiting my comeback. When I don't respond to the insult, he smiles sadly. "I can't afford to baby you. This is a serious business, no room for lies or acts. When you were an average child, you could afford to be a coward — nobody suffered. Now you have to be a hero or untold billions might die."

"That's an exaggeration, isn't it?" I mutter.

"No. Those are the stakes we play for. If it was hundreds, it wouldn't matter — I let that many die on the plane. Even millions . . . the world can afford to lose a few million humans every now and again. You could think of it as judicious pruning. Mankind would continue whether you joined us or not.

"But we deal in *billions* — wholesale slaughter. If the more powerful Demonata make it through, everybody perishes.

That's why you can't be a coward any longer. I won't let you deny your calling just because you're a nice boy and I feel sorry for you. We have a duty — me, Kernel, you. Fair or not, that's the way it is. So you're coming through that window with us. Unless the coward within you is stronger than I think . . ."

He looks at me harshly. Behind him, Kernel keeps his head down. I think he's ashamed of Beranabus, but also of himself and the choices the pair of them must make. The choice *I* must make.

"I can't do it." I sob. "You don't understand. I've replayed those battles with Lord Loss so many times . . . Vein and Artery . . . *Slawter* . . . the anguish. I did it the first time to save Bill-E, because he's my brother, and in Slawter because we were trapped and it was fight or die. But there was never time to worry about it in advance or make a considered decision to pit myself against demons. This is different. I'd be *choosing* horror and misery. I've seen the nightmarish work of the Demonata in real life and in dreams. I can't face them again. I *can't*."

"You can," Beranabus says, not giving up. "Unless you want to accept that you're a worthless coward. Unless you're prepared to flee like a whipped, shamed cur. Are you, Grubitsch?"

"I . . ." My voice seizes. I come within a breath of saying yes. I want to. I almost grasp the yellow mantle gratefully. But the shame . . . the guilt . . . to live the rest of my life as a branded coward . . .

"Please," I moan. "Don't do this to me."

"It's already done," Beranabus says. "I'm not pushing you into anything. I'm just the one who has the unpleasant task of breaking the news to you." He steps forward, grabs my shoulder, and looks hard into my eyes. "Hero or coward. There's no in between. Choose now. The Demonata won't wait forever."

Wanting to scream, to run, to tell him to go stuff himself. Knowing I can't, that I'm gifted, that I'm damned.

"I hope they kill me," I cry, tearing away from him, trembling wildly. "I hope I don't last five minutes."

"I hoped that too when I first crossed," Kernel says softly, then walks to the monolith, puts a hand on the surface, breathes on it, and steps through as the dark face shimmers. He vanishes.

"You will fare better than you fear, Grubitsch," Beranabus says encouragingly, following Kernel to the monolith. He puts a hand on it.

"Wait." I stop him and he looks back questioningly. "If we're going to do this, I want to make one thing clear. It's Grubbs, understand? I bloody hate *Grubitsch.*"

Beranabus smiles crookedly and says with all the charm of Sweeney Todd, "If you can kill demons, I'll call you anything you please. If not, I'll leave your bones lying scattered in their universe, nameless." He faces the monolith again and exhales. It shimmers and he moves forward. Gone.

I don't think about this being my chance to run, to get out of here, lose myself in the desert and die on my own world. Afraid the coward within me will take control if I give it a chance. Without hesitation, I lurch forward, put both hands on the monolith, breathe on it like the others did, and step through into madness.

# THE STUFF THAT
# HEROES ARE MADE OF

✠      ✠      ✠

FIRST impression — this place is infinitely different from
the webby world of Lord Loss. Light blue in color, it's like
something out of a Picasso painting, all cubes and weird angles. We're in a sort of valley. Narrow, jagged pillars of a
weird blue substance rise high around us. I edge over to the
nearest pillar and sniff, expecting the stench of sulfur. But it
smells more like a piece of rotten fruit — a peach or pear
maybe.

"Don't touch it," Beranabus says. "It's probably not dangerous, but we don't take chances here. The less physical
contact we make, the better."

"Where is this?" I ask.

"The Demonata's universe, idiot," Kernel snaps.

"I mean, which part? I don't know anything about the
setup here. Are there ten worlds, twenty, a thousand? Do
they have names? Which one are we on?"

"Geography doesn't work like that here," Beranabus says,
studying the pillars, eyes sharp. "The worlds and zones are

constantly changing. There are many self-contained galaxies within the general demon universe. The stronger Demonata have the power to create their own realms or take over another demon's and reshape it. We never know what we're going to find when we cross."

"Then how do you hunt?" I frown.

"We target specific demons. Realms might change but demons don't, except for the shape-shifters, and even they don't change on the inside, where it counts. If we know a demon's name, Kernel can locate it within minutes. If we don't know, or if the demon doesn't have a name, it's more complicated. Each demon has a unique spiritual vibration."

"Call it a demonic frequency," Kernel chips in when I look blank. "Demons have souls, like humans, and they emit a certain type of wave that we can sense. Each demon's soul is like a radio station, transmitting on an individual frequency. If we think a certain demon's working on a window or tunnel, we can lock on to its signal and track it down."

"It's not easy," Beranabus says, "especially if it's a demon we've had no firsthand experience of, but we usually find what we're looking for."

Kernel points to one of the shorter pillars. "There."

Beranabus squints. "Are you sure?"

"Positive."

"Either you're getting sharper or my eyes are getting worse," Beranabus mutters, then raises a hand and sends a ball of energy shooting at the pillar. There's a gentle glowing. A sound somewhere between a sigh and a moan. Then the *pillar* moves and an angular demon steps out of a crack.

Fear grabs hold and magic flares within me. I bring up my hands defensively, but Beranabus stops me with a high-spirited "Rein in those horses, boy!" He faces the demon and smiles. "How do you feel about dying today?"

The demon makes a series of choking noises. The sounds don't make sense to me but Beranabus can decipher them. "No," he says. "We're not going to leave you alone. You know who we are and what we want. Now, do you have something to tell us or do we make life wickedly uncomfortable for you?"

The demon glares at Beranabus through a series of triangular eyes, but it looks more miserable than angry. It's an odd creature, not really frightening in manner or appearance. It mutters something. Beranabus and Kernel share a glance. "You're sure?" Kernel asks, and the demon nods stiffly.

"Excellent." Beranabus beams and cocks his head at Kernel. The bald teenager shuffles away a couple of yards, then starts moving his hands about in the air. It's as if he's sliding invisible blocks around.

"What's happening?" I ask Beranabus quietly, not wanting to disturb Kernel.

"I'm opening a window," Kernel answers before Beranabus can, an edge to his voice. "This is my specialty. I can see panels of light that are invisible to all others. When I slide certain panels together, windows form. I can get to anywhere in this universe — or ours — through them."

"Where will this one lead?" I ask.

"You'll find out soon," Kernel says. "We're going in search of prey. You want to kill demons, don't you?"

"No. But let's say I did. What about that one?" I point to the blue demon, which is edging back into the crack, becoming one with the landscape again.

"Not worth killing," Beranabus says dismissively. "There are untold billions of demons. They're all evil, but most can't hurt us or cross to our world. That cretin doesn't even dare leave this valley. It waits, hiding and surviving, doing precious little else."

"What does it feed on?" I ask.

"Who knows?" Beranabus sniffs. "Maybe nothing. Most demons don't need to eat and drink. Many do, but out of choice, not necessity."

"Then why did we come here, if not to kill it?" I frown.

"Information," Kernel says, looking around. "We're like detectives with a team of snitches. We know where to find soft demons. We often come to places like this, rough up the locals, find out if anything foul is afoot — something usually is. Demons like that one might not do much, but they know things. Secrets are hard to keep in this universe. Word spreads quickly."

"What's the *word* now?" I ask, caught off guard. I don't know what I expected, but it wasn't something like this.

"There's a demon trying to possess a woman on Earth," Beranabus says. "That happens all the time. It's not a problem for us, though it's bad for those involved. Some demons who can't cross universes can establish a hold on the minds of humans. They manipulate them, drive them crazy, use them to create as much chaos as possible. We normally wouldn't bother with small-scale melodramatics like this, but I want to break you in gently."

Kernel grunts. "On *my* first mission we fought a pair of demons who had almost broken through to the center of Moscow. They were two of the toughest I've ever faced. It was bloody and tight. That's when I lost the tips of my fingers." He stares at his left hand, the fingers flinching inward as he relives the memory.

"Why couldn't you replace them?" I ask. "You can do that with magic, right?"

"Normally. But the loss made little difference. I decided to leave them as they were. They remind me of the dangers we face, the fact that success isn't a guarantee, that we can and will perish in this hellhole eventually."

"Here we go," Beranabus says briskly. A purplish window has formed in front of Kernel. Beranabus walks up to it and steps through, not bothering to breathe on this one. Kernel curls his fingers into a fist, then relaxes his fingers and follows.

I look back in the direction of the blue demon, but I can't see it now, even though I know the exact spot where it's hiding. Shaking my head, I think, "This isn't so bad. I can handle this." But I know it's a false start, that worse — much worse — is to come.

There's a sound far overhead, from the meteor-sized demons in the sky. Fearful of being attacked while I'm alone, I rush to the window and push through after the others.

✠ *Fire!* It's all around me, fierce, intense, out of control. I feel the hair on my arms singe and know I have only seconds before I burst into flames. Total panic. I want to look for

Beranabus and Kernel or scream for help, but my eyes and mouth shut automatically against the heat.

"Oh, for the love of . . ." Kernel tuts, taking hold of my arm and shaking it roughly. "This is ridiculous. He's not ready for this. Send him back."

"He'll learn," Beranabus says, and then his lips are by my left ear. "Use magic to guide yourself."

"It's hell!" I moan, speaking out of the side of my mouth, keeping my eyes shut.

"One of many thousands of hells," Beranabus grunts. "For every imaginative demon who constructs a terrifyingly original realm, there are scores who draw upon tired old human myths. Stop acting like a fool. You can already feel your magic responding to this, protecting you from the flames. You'd be burning to a crisp right now if not."

I open one eye, then the other. Nothing to see but flames. Beranabus and Kernel are hard to spot among the flickering licks of yellow and red. Still hot, hotter than I should be able to bear. But magic's humming away in the background, cooling me down, guarding my freckled flesh. Beranabus is right — it kicked in as soon as I set foot here, even as the hairs on my arms began to shrivel. I knew that — I could feel it — but fear made me panic.

"Where's the demon?" I ask, trying to peer through the walls of fire. I look down and realize we're truly in the middle of the flames — no floor. Nothing below, above, or to the sides except fire.

"The flames *are* the demon," Kernel says. "It's a universal demon."

"Am I supposed to know what that means?" I growl.

"Universal demons don't just inhabit a galaxy of their own — they become it," Beranabus explains. "This demon has a fascination with fire, so it became flames. Its whole zone — the demon itself — is made of fire."

"But where does it start?" I ask. "Where does it end?"

"Nowhere," Beranabus says. "This demon is its own self-contained and at the same time limitless realm. It's like our universe — infinite."

While I'm trying to make sense of that — I've always had problems thinking of a universe being infinite, never mind one single creature — the flames thicken around us. There's a horrible shrieking sound, piercing and destructive. My eardrums and eyeballs should burst, but magic protects me instinctively. (Which is just as well, since I wouldn't know how to start to control it!)

A shape forms amid the flames, gigantic and bulging, like the wizard's fake head in *The Wizard of Oz*, only a hundred times bigger and more frightening, full of leaping shadows, sparks, and flames.

The demon shrieks again. A huge, rough, fiery fist forms and smashes down on Beranabus. He waves an arm at the fist and slices through the flames. The edges of his beard singe but he's otherwise unharmed.

Another fist forms and tries to swat Kernel aside. He leaps high, somersaults over it, opens his mouth midleap, and sucks in sharply. He inhales flames, face turning a pure, angry, painful white. The demon screams. Kernel lands, coughs, spins, and leaps over another quickly formed fist.

Beranabus grabs handfuls of flames and rams them into his stomach. And I mean *into* — his hands pierce his own flesh. He's stuffing his guts full of fire. The hands come out, the wall of his stomach unharmed. He grabs more flames and jams them in. Out — in. Out — in.

And what does the *heroic* Grubbs Grady do? I hang beside them, helpless and shivering, about as much use as a plastic toasting fork. I want to help, but I don't know how. My magic isn't strong enough. I don't want to be here. This isn't my fight.

Then, in the middle of the battle, the demon focuses on me. Two huge fists form on either side and slam toward me, to hammer me lifeless.

I throw myself to the floor. Except there isn't a floor. Just flames. I don't know how I've been hovering, but I'm not anymore. I'm falling, like when Beranabus ripped me out of the plane, dropping like a sack of stones, quickly losing sight of the magician and his assistant.

"Help!" I scream.

"Help yourself," Beranabus roars, then curses brutally.

I come to a stop. Relief evaporates moments later when I realize I haven't been helped by Beranabus or Kernel — I'm being held in the middle of a giant hand of fire. The fingers close upon me. The heat's unbearable. I feel my magic struggling, protesting, pleading with me to direct it, use it, fight back. But what can I do? How can I defeat a creature made of flames? It's impossible. At least Lord Loss and his familiars were real targets. I could hit them. This is lunacy. We're all going to perish, burned to death by a demon the size of a universe.

I scream at the flames. The fingers stop, shudder, then tear apart. I fall again. I'm crying, taking no satisfaction out of destroying the hand because I'm sure another will form any second now, bigger, stronger, hotter.

Then Kernel is by my side. His eyes are sharp and bright blue with rage. "Bloody amateur," he sneers. "Bloody coward."

"I can't do it," I babble. "I told you I couldn't. I didn't want to come here. Make me stop falling. Help me get —"

"Shut up, you worm!" Kernel shouts. "I should let you burn." He laughs cruelly. "The hell with it. Your death would serve no purpose." He darts away from me, angling down, moving much quicker than I'm falling. He becomes a speck, then stops. As I hurtle toward him, I see his hands moving, the way they did when he created the window to this universe.

When I'm maybe a few hundred feet away, a dark green window forms. Kernel slides away from it and waves at me like a policeman directing traffic. I'm rushing toward the window. The flames peel away from me. The window gets bigger and bigger as I fall upon it. I have just enough time to worry about what will happen when I flash through and smash into the ground on the other side. Then I hit it and everything turns green.

# A FACE FROM THE PAST

✠   ✠   ✠

I LAND hard on the floor of Beranabus's cave, but no bones shatter. Groaning, I pick myself up and look around. The fire has burned out — only cold ashes remain. But flashlights glow on the walls, the flames kept alive by magic. Overhead the window hangs flat, six feet or so above me. A few moments later, as I'm edging clear of it on my hands and knees, it shimmers, then breaks apart and disappears.

I crawl to my blanket and lie down, panting, heart still racing from my encounter with the fire demon, bones aching from the impact of the fall. I shut my eyes and shiver, then climb beneath the blanket for warmth.

Lying in the gloom and quiet. Thinking about the universe of the Demonata. My eyes open and tears wet my lashes. I'm ashamed. I acted like a gutless coward. What's happened to me? I was braver than this when I faced Lord Loss. Scared, but I fought bravely. Why can't I be that way now? For long hours I lie still, pondering, before falling into a troubled, restless, shame-tinged sleep.

✠ ✠ ✠

✠ No sign of Beranabus and Kernel when I wake. I worry about them for a few minutes but then recall them saying time usually passes faster here than in the universe of the Demonata. A fight that lasts an hour or two there can equate to days, weeks, or even months here.

Rising stiffly, I explore the cave in search of food and water. I find ample supplies stacked in all corners, the food imperishable, the water carefully bottled. So I won't starve or die of thirst. Not unless they're gone for *years* . . .

The fire next. There are logs and chunks of turf nearby but no matches or lighters. I try one of the flashlights, but they're secured tight to the wall and I don't want to break any off. I guess Beranabus and Kernel use magic to start the fire. Reluctant to disturb my inner powers, I attempt to play caveman and ignite the fire by rubbing sticks together, banging a couple of stones off each other in search of an elusive first spark. But I quickly discover that I'm nowhere near as advanced as a caveman.

Sitting back, frowning at the logs. It's not especially cold in the cave, but I want to light a fire regardless, more for the comfort of its crackling, natural flames than anything else. So, cautiously, I reach within myself and look for magic. But it withdraws as I come near. I sense the power, but it darts out of reach. I feel like it's punishing me, annoyed that I didn't use it to fight the demon. *You can go stuff yourself if you think I'll help you now! Make your own fire, coward!*

Giving up, I grab a can of beans, a fork, and a can opener and return to my blanket, where I eat the beans cold. Staring at the lifeless fire as I eat. Remembering the flames in the other universe and my cowardice. Trying to justify my actions. What was I meant to do? Suck in flames like Kernel? Jam them into my gut like Beranabus? If they'd shown me how, I could have. But they dropped me into it, no warnings or advice. Maybe I wasn't really a coward, just ignorant.

Unable to convince myself. If we'd been fighting a demon master, I could plead inexperience. But Kernel said this was a lesser demon. Beranabus was starting me off lightly, testing me out on one of the meeker monsters. There can be no excuses.

I lurch to my feet. I'm getting out of here. I don't want to be around when they return. I'll hide my shame in the desert. Take off, let the sun roast me or the chill night air freeze me. Die alone and lost. No more worries or cares. Better off out of this insane game of werewolves, magic, and demons.

I rush to the rope ladder and haul myself up, muscles pumping. Going so fast, I smack my skull on the roof of the cave when I get to the top. Wincing, I rub my head and retreat a couple of rungs, then look for the opening. I can't find one. The rock appears to be solid. I run my fingers over it, searching for a crack or button, but there's nothing. It must open by magic.

Descending sourly. Hating magic all the more. Why can't I be an ordinary teen with normal problems? I never looked for magic. Wasn't the least bit interested in it. So why did it pick on me? What the hell have I done to deserve this?

Back to my blanket. Glaring at the cold embers of the fire. Waiting impatiently for Beranabus and Kernel's return. Half wishing I'd stayed in the Demonata's universe and fried.

✠ ✠ ✠

✠ Time passes slowly, miserably. No way of telling if it's day or night. When I'm not sleeping, I just sit and think, eat mechanically, or walk in circles around the cave. Go to the back and dig a hole when I need the toilet, then fill it in. Disgusted the first few times, but now it's second nature. No biggie.

I often find myself wondering what's happening in the other universe, wishing I could find the courage to go back, rejoin the fight, and redeem myself. Playing out all manner of wild scenarios inside my head, in which I'm Grubbs Grady — superhero. I find Beranabus and Kernel in dire straits, backs against a fiery wall, at the mercy of the demon. It's laughing evilly, about to finish them off. Then I lay into it and rip it to pieces. I shout at the startled Beranabus and Kernel, "You didn't think I'd run away, did you? I just had to visit the men's room." They cheer as I kill the demon, then rush to clap my back, sing my praises, hail me as a savior.

Nice dreams. But completely unconnected to reality. Because for all the wishing and make-believe, I don't know how to open a window to the demon's universe. And I'm certain, beyond any shadow of a doubt, that even if one materialized in front of me, I wouldn't have the guts to step through. A hero only inside my head. In the real world I remain a coward.

✠ Snapping out of a typically disturbed sleep. There are heavy, thumping noises. I think it's Beranabus and Kernel returning or a demon breaking through. But when I look around there's nothing in the cave. I frown, wondering if the noises were part of the dream. Listen for ages, sitting up. Silence.

I try to sleep again but I'm too unsettled. So I walk around the cave for the millionth time. After a while I jog. Twenty laps, followed by push-ups, squats, more jogging. Shadow-punching as I run. Knocking hordes of imaginary monsters out.

A series of short sprints. In better physical condition than I've been in a long time — maybe ever. Thinking about Loch and how approving he'd be if he could see me now. He was always pushing me to exercise more. Said I was a mountain of muscles that hadn't been honed, that I could be truly ferocious if I pushed myself to my limits. But I never bothered. There was always something better to do with my time.

Not anymore. This is how Olympians should train. Shut themselves off from the world in a musky, murky cave, with nothing to do except exercise. Works wonders when it comes to concentration. If I ever get out of here, maybe that will be my true calling in life — coach to athletic stars. It would certainly beat the hell out of killing demons for a living!

✠ Still exercising. I've been at it for hours, pausing only for periods of short rest and to eat. Sweating so much, I have to take my clothes off. Keeping only my boxers on, in case Beranabus and Kernel drop in without warning.

Suddenly, I hear the noises again. Three heavy thumps, a pause, three more. Then silence.

I come to a standstill, listening to the echoes of the thumps. They came from overhead — the closed entrance to the cave. With sudden hope in my heart, I race to the ladder and scurry to the top, where I wait a few seconds for more sounds. When there's only silence, I roar, "Hello!" and listen again. Nothing.

Back to the bottom of the ladder. I look for something to strike the roof of the cave with, but there's not much here. I go through the drawers of Beranabus's table — the first time I've examined it — but there's nothing except papers, pens, and small knickknacks. I note absentmindedly that the flowers are still blooming, fresh as ever.

Eventually, I grab one of the longer logs from the woodpile and drag it up the ladder, then pound the roof with it, three times, a pause, then three more. I hold it by my side, trying to stifle my heavy breathing so I can hear clearly, praying for a series of answering knocks. But there aren't any.

I pound the roof again and again without reply. Eventually, I give up and drop the log. I hang there a while longer, then climb down, dejected. Halfway to the floor I realize that if the noises were human-made, maybe the person has left. When there was no immediate answer, maybe he or she decided there was nobody home, that they'd try again later.

Back on the ground, I drink half a bottle of water, go to the toilet, then return to the base of the ladder, pick up the log, and climb again. At the top I settle back, get as comfortable as I can, and wait, desperate to make contact with another human being.

✠ Many hours later. My legs and arms ache from clinging to the ladder. Tired and irritated. Telling myself I'm wasting my time. The noises were probably a rockfall. I should climb down, get some sleep, then fill the hours with more exercise.

On the point of quitting when the noises come again — three resounding thumps, a pause, then three more, just like earlier. In a fit of excitement I raise the log — then drop it! Reacting swiftly, I grab for it, catch it, and arc it upward, slamming it hard into the roof of the cave, once, twice, three times. A short pause before I hammer the roof again. Then, heart beating hard, I lower it and listen.

Nothing.

For several minutes I hang there, hopeful, awaiting an answer. But as the silence stretches I realize there's not going to be one. Either the thuds are the result of an especially large animal or the rock overhead is too thick for the noises I make to carry to the other side. Perhaps they're using magic to penetrate the rock sheet, or maybe they have an especially large hammer.

Dejected, I descend, then head for my blanket and the escape of sleep. Even my nightmares are more welcome than the monotony of the cave.

�֍ More empty hours follow, the only distraction — apart from exercise — coming in the form of the thumping noises at regular intervals. I'm sure it's a person — no animal could make the same sounds over and over — but with no way of contacting them, I lose interest and soon stop wondering who it might be. After a while I even start to ignore the thumps and barely notice them when they come.

Then, one day — or night — as I'm halfway through a four-minute sprint, a green window forms close to the remains of the fire and Kernel steps through. I come to a halt almost directly in front of him. He stares at me icily, casts a curious eye over my bare chest and legs, then goes to the fire and starts it with a single word.

As I'm pulling my clothes on, Beranabus appears. His beard is badly burned and his hands are red, but otherwise he's unharmed. "Been keeping the cave warm for us?" he says sneeringly.

"He didn't even manage to get the fire going," Kernel snorts.

"Why doesn't that surprise me?"

"Did you . . . the demon . . . is it . . . ?" I mutter.

"All taken care of," Beranabus says. "Quenched forever, its universe now a cold, lifeless expanse of space. Human saved, order restored, tragedy averted."

"No thanks to *you*," Kernel sniffs.

I ignore the insult. "How long were you in there?"

"No idea," Beranabus says as the window behind him vanishes. "It felt like a day. What about here?"

"A couple of weeks. Maybe three."

"That must have been boring."

"Serves him right," Kernel snaps, shooting me a disgusted look. "Running out like that . . . leaving us to deal with it ourselves . . ."

"It's not like we had to struggle," Beranabus murmurs, no idea that his kindness makes me feel worse than ever.

"He didn't have to know that," Kernel hisses. "He left us to fight alone. Didn't stop to think if we might need him. Didn't care."

"That's not true," I say sullenly. "Yes, I ran. But I did care.

I just couldn't . . . it was too . . . I told you!" I cry. "I didn't want to go. You made me."

"Listen to him," Kernel jeers. "He sounds like a five-year-old. I wouldn't have thought someone his age and size could be so gutless. Maybe he —"

"Enough!" Beranabus barks. Sighing, he heads to his table and motions me to follow. He sits on an old wooden chair, stretches his legs out, cracks his knuckles above his head, and yawns. Lowering his hands, he fiddles with some of the flowers, shuffles papers around, then takes a drawing out of one of the drawers and stares at it.

"I'm sorry," I say softly.

"No," he sighs. "It was my fault. I thought you were made of stronger stuff. I could see the fear in you and your reluctance to get involved. But given your background, I thought you'd shrug it off once faced with a demon, that you'd rise to the occasion like you did before."

"It was different then," I tell him. "I didn't know what I was getting into the first time, and in Slawter I was trapped. I had no choice but to fight. I've had so many horrible nights since then, so many nightmares. I'm not just scared of demons now — I'm bloody terrified."

"I understand," Beranabus says. "I didn't before, but I do now." He studies the drawing again, then lays it aside. "I'm a poor judge of character. I've made mistakes before, taken children into the universe of the Demonata when they weren't ready, lost them cheaply. But they've always been fighters. This is the first time I've taken someone who lacked the stomach for battle. It was a grave error on my part. I should have known better."

"You're not mad at me?"

"No. I'm sad. You have such ability, it's a shame to see it go to waste. But if the fighting instinct isn't there, there's no point moping. I thought you were a warrior. I was wrong. You don't criticize a pony for not being a horse."

He falls silent and looks around at the flowers on the table. I'm not sure I like his comparison. Never thought of myself as Grubbs Grady — pony! But I guess it's appropriate. I might lack the guts to be a hero, but at least I have pride enough not to whine when the truth is pointed out.

"What happens now?" I ask.

"Hmm?"

"I can't fight. So what happens? Will you take me back? Set me loose in the desert? What?"

Beranabus frowns. "I can't spare much time. You wouldn't survive outside, and it would be cruel to make you wait here indefinitely. I'll take you to the nearest human outpost. You'll have to make your own way from there. Once you get home, tell Dervish what happened. Ask him to help you work on your magic. Even if you can't fight, you can watch for demons. Become a Disciple. I know you'd rather keep out of this completely, but you might make a difference. Do you think you could do that?"

"Sure," I gush, delighted to be told I'm not entirely worthless. "I avoided magic because I thought if I learned it, I'd have to fight demons. But if I just have to be a watchdog . . ."

"Good choice of words," Kernel snorts.

"Now, now," Beranabus says. "Let's not be ungracious."

Kernel spits into the fire. His spit sizzles, revealing more about his opinion of me than he could ever say with words.

"When do we leave?" I ask, eager to be out of here, free of this confining cave and Kernel's scorn.

"Soon," Beranabus promises. "I need to get some sleep, and eat when I wake, but after that we'll depart."

"Great." I grin, turning away to let the elderly magician go to rest. Then I remember the noises and turn to tell him. "I forgot, somebody's been . . ."

I come to a halt. Beranabus is leaning over, stroking the leaves of one of the flowers, smiling fondly at it. I can see the drawing he was looking at earlier. It's a pencil sketch of a girl's face. And though the paper is yellow and wrinkled with age, the face is shockingly familiar.

"Who's that?" I croak. Beranabus looks up questioningly. I point a trembling finger at the drawing. "The girl — who is she?"

"Someone who died a very long time ago," Beranabus says, touching the paper. "She sacrificed her life fighting the Demonata, to keep the world safe. An example to us all. Not that I'm trying to make you feel small. I didn't mean —"

"There was a voice," I interrupt, eyes fixed on the drawing. "At the cave in Carcery Vale. I didn't mention it before — it didn't seem to matter and there was so much else to tell you. But when I went to the cave, I heard a voice and saw a face in the rocks. It was alive. Even though it was in the rock, it could open its eyes and move its lips. It spoke to me."

I pick up the drawing and study the girl's face, the curve of her jaw, the eyes and mouth. "This is the girl from the cave. She called to me . . . warned me, I think, but I don't know what of. She spoke in a different lan —"

"It can't be!" Beranabus snaps, snatching the drawing back. "This girl has been dead for almost sixteen hundred years. You're mistaken."

"No," I say certainly. "It was her. I'm sure of it. Who the hell was she, and why did she try so hard to contact me?"

In answer to that, Beranabus only sits and stares at me, shocked — and *afraid*.

# THE WARNING

✛   ✛   ✛

**I**MPOSSIBLE!" Beranabus keeps croaking. "Impossible!" He's striding around the cave, hair and eyes even wilder than normal, clutching the drawing of the girl to his chest, muttering to himself, occasionally bursting out with another round of, "Impossible! Impossible!"

Kernel and I have drawn together by the fire, temporarily united by our uncertainty. "Has he ever gone off like this before?" I whisper.

"No," Kernel replies quietly. "He often talks to himself, but I've never seen him so agitated."

"Do you know who the girl is?"

Kernel shakes his head. "Just some old drawing that he gets out every now and then and moons over."

"Beranabus said she died sixteen hundred years ago."

"I heard."

"Do you think he knew her? Was he alive then?"

"No." Kernel frowns. "He couldn't have been. We can live a long time, battling the Demonata in their universe, even a few hundred years. But no human can live that long. At least that's what Beranabus taught me."

Beranabus stops pacing, whirls, and fixes his stare on me. "You!" he shouts. "Come here!" I glance at Kernel for support. "Don't waste my time! Get over here now!"

Since I don't want to enrage him any further, I edge across but keep out of immediate reach. Beranabus holds the drawing up. His hands are shaking. "How sure are you?" he growls.

"It's her," I tell him. "The girl in the cave. I'm certain."

"Would you stake your life on it?" he snarls.

"No," I say hesitantly. "But it *is* her. You don't forget a face like that. It's not every day a person speaks to you from within the heart of a rock."

Beranabus lowers the drawing. Turns it around so he can study the face again. "You say she's alive?" he asks, voice low.

I shrug. "She spoke to me. But it wasn't a real face. It was a cross between flesh and stone. She could have been some sort of ghost, I guess."

"Of course," Beranabus says. "But a ghost imprisoned *there* . . . trapped all this time . . ." His eyes shoot up. "Tell me what she said."

"I can't. I didn't understand her. She spoke a different language."

"Don't be stupid! You can . . ." He stops and gets his breathing under control. "First things first. Tell me the whole story. Everything this time. About the cave, what you saw and heard. Leave nothing out."

I don't want to go through it again, but he's not going to tell me anything until I do, so I quickly trot out the story, filling in all the details I skipped the first time. Seeing the face in the rock. The eyes opening. Later, when the girl spoke to me. In the cave, the night of my turning, when she screamed at me and seemed to be trying to warn me.

"Warn you of what?" Beranabus asks.

"Maybe that Juni was a traitor. Or of the danger Bill-E was in."

"Perhaps," Beranabus mutters. "There are blood ties between you that might account for her interest in your predicament, but to break out of the rock and make herself heard must have required a huge amount of energy and effort. Why would she do that just to save your lives?"

He's not expecting an answer, so I don't try to provide one. Instead, I pick up on something else he said and ask stiffly, "What blood ties?"

He waves a hand as though it's nothing. "The girl was called Bec. A distant ancestor of yours."

*"Ancestor?"*

"A distant one," he repeats. "She was a priestess . . . a magician. A brave, true, selfless girl."

"Did you know her?" Kernel asks. He's slightly behind us, listening closely. "Were you alive then?"

"I'd be a real Methuselah if so," Beranabus says. He looks at the drawing again and frowns. "I need to know what she said. She might have simply been trying to help you, but I think there's more to it. We need to study her words."

"But I told you, I couldn't understand her. I don't speak her language."

"I do," Beranabus says, then gestures to the chair behind the desk. "I'm going to teach you another remembering spell, like the one we used to prove you didn't kill your brother's grandparents. But with this one you'll repeat everything the girl said. I'll be able to translate."

I sit. Beranabus clears an area of the table, then lays the drawing down gently, so it's facing me. "Look into her eyes," he says softly. "Forget everything that's happened recently. Let your mind drift back." He gives me a minute, then says, "Repeat after me."

I mimic Beranabus's words carefully. As the spell develops, the lines on the paper shimmer. I'm startled, but I've seen a lot more incredible stuff in my time, so I don't lose concentration. The lines begin to move. The face doesn't bulge out of the page the way it projected from the rocks, but it comes alive. The eyes flicker and the lips part. The girl talks. No sounds come, just the motions. But as the spell concludes and Beranabus stops talking, I find my own lips moving in time with the drawing's. Only it's not my voice — it's the girl's.

I speak swiftly, anxiously, the muscles of my throat hurting from having to form such unusual words. I spot Kernel listening with a frown, unable to interpret. But Beranabus understands perfectly. And the more I say, the more his face pales and he trembles.

Before I finish, the elderly magician sinks to the floor and stares at me, appalled. I want to ask him what the girl said, but I can't. My lips continue to move and the dead girl's words spill out. I'm repeating myself from the beginning.

Beranabus groans and covers his ears with his hands. "No," he wheezes. "Gods be damned. *No!*"

"Beranabus?" Kernel says, approaching his master cautiously. "What's wrong?"

"His fault!" Beranabus shrieks, pointing an accusing finger at me. "If he'd told me when he first came here . . ." He shakes his head and curses. I carry on talking, unable to stop. I'm afraid he's going to leave me this way, that I'll warble on like this forever.

Finally, rising slowly, Beranabus growls something and the words cease. My mouth closes. I rub my aching jaws and throat, staring at the magician, wondering what I've done to infuriate him.

"Damn you, Grubitsch Grady," he says bitterly, shooing me out of his chair and lowering himself into it, picking up the drawing and cradling it to his chest. There are angry, hopeless tears in his eyes. "Damn the day you came into this world. If I'd known the trouble you'd cause, I'd have killed you at birth, you meddling, cowardly, destructive brat."

"Beranabus!" Kernel gasps as my insides clench tight.

"It's true!" Beranabus shouts. "I stood up for the wretched fool, but I shouldn't have. I should have just . . . just . . ." He stops, closes his eyes, and moans. "No. You didn't know what you were doing. I can't blame you."

"I don't care what you think of me," I snap, angry and ashamed. "Just tell me what she said, you horrible old buzzard."

Beranabus opens his eyes and smiles faintly. "That's more like it, boy. Spirit." His smile disappears. "Bec *was* trying to warn you, but she wasn't interested in saving your life. The stakes were much higher. She . . ."

He clears his throat, then continues lifelessly. "I don't know how she wound up where she is or how she managed to communicate with you, but her soul has been trapped in that cave since she died, torn between life and death, between our universe and the Demonata's. I've never seen that before. Ghosts, aye, but only pale shades of those who died. This is different. She somehow defied the laws of death and her soul remains intact. It shouldn't . . ." He coughs and shakes his head, then continues.

"Bec is able to peer into the demon universe from where she's trapped. She's been observing the Demonata for centuries. She became aware long ago of a powerful demon master trying to open a tunnel to this world. When she sensed you clearing the entrance to the cave, she was afraid the creature would learn of it and restore the ancient tunnel. That's why she tried to warn you off. Later she learned of a more direct threat, which is why she appeared so desperate the last time she established contact.

"I made a fatal error. I thought Lord Loss wasn't interested in opening a tunnel between the two universes. But he's changed his views. When Dervish told Juni about the cave, her master decided to kill two birds with one stone. His plan was to slaughter you, Dervish, and your brother — or take you back to his own realm to torture — then open the tunnel, clearing the way for the ranks of demons to cross."

Beranabus pauses. Kernel and I are staring at him, dumbstruck.

"Juni must have made a sacrifice after Dervish revealed the cave to her," he goes on. "It takes a few weeks for the blood of a sacrificed victim to prime the tunnel walls. The spells of opening can't be cast until then. I was guarding the cave closely, but somehow she got in and killed someone without my knowledge.

"Lord Loss could have opened the tunnel at any time, but he decided to do it during a full moon, when there was more magic in the air. Tapping into the power of the moon, he could complete the spells within a few hours. That way, if I discovered him while he was at work, he'd only have to hold me at bay for that short time.

"Being a lover of neatness, he planned to kill or abduct you three and open the tunnel on the same night. Unfortunately for him, your magic burst to the surface and derailed things. He missed his chance to get even with the Grady clan at the cave. Since settling his score with you before he opened the floodgates was important to him, he pushed his plans back by a month."

"Then we still have time!" I gasp. "It's not too late. We know what he's going to do. We'll return to the cave and fight."

"*We?*" Kernel says sarcastically.

"Yes! I'll fight to save Dervish and Bill-E. I don't care what those monsters throw at us. When it's family, it's different."

"You really think you can choose not to be a coward if and when it suits you?" Kernel jeers.

Beranabus interrupts wearily before I can retort. "It doesn't matter. You're arguing about nothing. The time for heroics has passed."

"What are you talking about?" I say edgily.

"It's difficult to track time here," Beranabus says softly, "but not impossible. I can reach out and make a quick check on the heavens when I wish. I did that while Bec was speaking. You miscalculated, Grubbs. It's been seven weeks since I rescued you from the airplane."

I start to shiver. "But . . . no . . . maybe Lord Loss delayed again. He wanted to kill me before he opened the tunnel, but I'm still alive. Maybe —"

"No," Beranabus stops me. "Once I'd established the date, I cast my senses further afield. When there's a rip of great magnitude between universes a magician can detect it. If the spells I'd cast at the cave worked, I'd have known earlier. I should have renewed them, but it seemed like there was no rush. I wouldn't have made that mistake a hundred years ago. I'm getting so old. . . ."

Beranabus sighs and his head drops. "The demons crossed as planned. They've had three weeks to stabilize, multiply, and spread. Your town is theirs. Probably your country too. Dervish . . . your brother . . . everybody else you know in Carcery Vale . . ." He finishes in an awful whisper that fills me with a dread beyond any I've ever experienced. "The Demonata have had their way with them. They're all dead now — and probably millions more besides."

# PART TWO

✠  ✠  ✠

# BEC-E

# THE MESSENGER

✠ ✠ ✠

EVERYBODY in the Vale — dead. Unable to believe it. I want to scream my head off, call Beranabus a liar, demand he tell the truth. Except . . . I can *see* the truth in the old magician's eyes. In his stooped shoulders. In his weariness as he sets his papers in order and prepares to leave for Carcery Vale to find out how far the Demonata have spread. He wasn't lying. They really did break through. Dervish and Bill-E are . . .

I don't complete the thought. Filled with sickness and fear. The last time I felt this empty inside was when I lost my parents and sister. It took me months to recover, and that was only with Dervish's help. Now I'm alone, racked with guilt and shame as well as grief. I don't know if there's any way back. Madness looms, waiting to consume me. I doubt if I can fight it.

Kernel is sitting by the fire, staring glumly into the flames. Every so often he trembles as he thinks about the battle to come. He's been fighting demons for years, but in their universe, where his powers are far greater than they are here. On Earth his magical talents are vastly diminished. The Demonata are weaker here too, of course, and if it were just a few of them, he and Beranabus would fancy their chances. But if thousands have crossed and are running riot . . .

A sudden pounding noise. Three blows, a pause, then three more. Beranabus and Kernel jump nervously at the first sound, then relax.

"I forgot," I say quietly, madness receding temporarily, confident of taking me whenever it chooses. "Those noises have been coming for the past week. I went up the ladder to find out what was making them, but I couldn't get out."

"The entrance is protected by spells," Beranabus says. "Only Kernel and I can open it." He nods at Kernel, who heads for the ladder. "Be careful," Beranabus calls after him. "It might not be one of ours."

A short while later, Kernel returns. An elderly Indian woman in a light blue sari comes after him, limping but making good speed. She has a kind face, but it's twisted with worry. At first I don't know where I recognize her from. Then I remember — she was in a dream I had in Slawter last year.

"Sharmila," Beranabus greets her, smiling wanly.

"Master, there has been a tragic —" the woman begins in a rush.

"I know," Beranabus sighs. "The Demonata have crossed. I just found out. I'm going to Carcery Vale shortly, but perhaps you can flesh out the details before I leave."

The woman stares at Beranabus blankly. "You are going there?"

"I think I should," Beranabus says. "A stand must be made, aye?"

"But there are so many of them." The woman wheezes.

Beranabus frowns, then tilts his head at me. "This is Sharmila Mukherji, one of my Disciples. Sharmila, this is Grubitsch Grady — though I believe he prefers the name of Grubbs. He's Dervish's nephew."

Sharmila looks at me with surprising anger. "*Dervish!* He was on watch. He was supposed to make sure the tunnel was never reopened. He failed. He —"

"I don't believe in finger-pointing," Beranabus interrupts curtly, conveniently forgetting that he himself was pointing a finger at me not so long ago. "I trusted Dervish as much as I trust any of you. I'm sure he did all that anyone could. Now tell me how the situation stands. Quickly."

"There is no point," Sharmila snaps. "We have lost. They . . ." She stops and looks around the cave. Smiles briefly when she spots Kernel. Frowns when she faces Beranabus again. "I have been waiting in the upper cave for many days, incapable of contacting you. I told you years ago that you should share the access spells with us, so we could reach you swiftly in case of an emergency. It was probably too late even then, but if I had been able to find you directly . . ."

"It's easy to be wise in retrospect," Beranabus sniffs. "I made that call a long time ago and I stick by it, even now. It was essential that I remain protected from . . ." He trails off into silence, then growls to himself. "This is getting us nowhere. Tell me what's happening. *Please.*"

"I am not up to date with the latest developments," Sharmila replies sourly. "I was in contact with Shark until four days ago, but he broke the lines of communication. I suspect he lost patience and went into battle without you. He was never the most . . ."

She shrugs, then straightens her shoulders and speaks quickly. "The Demonata crossed three weeks ago in great numbers. They worked like soldiers, coordinated, attacking set targets, establishing control of the area around the cave. They have fractured since then, individuals branching off by themselves, spreading in chaotic directions. But they were organized to begin with. We did not expect that. They have never banded together in that way before. Who could have commanded them? Who has the power to unite so many monsters for even a short period of time?"

"It doesn't matter," Beranabus says. "The investigation can come later. Tell me more about the invasion. They were able to operate by day as well as night?"

"Most of them," Sharmila says. "There were some weaker demons, but most in the first wave were beasts of great strength. The sun meant nothing to them."

"Strange," Beranabus frowns. "They can't have massed in advance — I would have received word of such a buildup long ago. They must have been summoned when the cave was reactivated. But for so many to gather so quickly . . . You're right. This was no ordinary attack. There was a leader working behind the scenes, establishing contacts, making allies, forging secret links, priming them to await a call, so they could respond immediately."

He shudders. "It's our worst fear come true. The disorderly division between the Demonata has always been our strongest card. But if they've finally found a figurehead to unite and lead them . . ." He puts the thought aside and nods sharply at Sharmila to continue.

"They established control of Carcery Vale and the nearby regions within a day," Sharmila says. "They expanded steadily over the next few days and nights, conquering neighboring towns and villages, establishing bases. Most people had fled their homes by then, but the demons did not care. They were more interested in boundaries than victims — again, very undemonlike behavior."

"Did anyone survive?" I ask, not wanting to interrupt but having to. "In Carcery Vale, were any spared?"

Sharmila laughs brutally. "Do not be ridiculous! It was a bloodbath. They kept a few alive to torture, but most were slaughtered that first day."

"But not all," I whisper, a faint ray of hope forming, forcing the madness back, giving me a ghost of a reason to stay sane. "Lord Loss hates Dervish and Bill-E. He wouldn't want to kill them quickly. Maybe he spared them, so he could torment them at his leisure."

"It doesn't matter," Beranabus says gruffly. "Alive or dead, it makes no difference, not when an army of demons separates us from them. Finish your report, Sharmila."

The Indian lady shrugs. "The rest should be obvious. Public shock, confusion, and denial to begin with. We live in scientific, enlightened times. People do not believe in demons. Even when the film crews went in and the first pictures emerged, most refused to accept it. They thought the pictures were computer generated, the work of a prankster, maybe an especially cunning film producer trying to generate interest in her next movie. There was talk of Davida Haym faking her death a year earlier in order to set this up. Quite ironic, no? But as the days went by, realization sank in. There were too many confirmed deaths, a never-ending series of reports, and no government denials."

"Bless the governments," Kernel snorts. "How did our great leaders respond?"

"Slowly," Sharmila says. "We warned them of the threat of the Demonata many times in the past, even though Beranabus told us not to bother."

"I've never met a politician who didn't deserve to be tossed into a pit full of Kallin," Beranabus grunts.

"Nobody heeded our warnings," Sharmila continues. "Despite all the evidence we presented and our predictions of what would happen if a prolonged invasion ever came to pass, we were treated as cranks. We have always had a number of supporters in various high-ranking corners of the globe, but not enough to make a difference.

"Most governments spent the initial week in a blind panic. First, they had to confirm that the reports were genuine — which took a few days. Then they debated the meaning of it, what the demons might want, how they could placate them, what their response should be if the demons refused to negotiate. A few acted quickly and sent troops in — mostly from nearby countries that could see they were next on the agenda — but it was the second week before the war began for real."

"War," Beranabus murmurs, face crinkling. "Most humans know nothing of true warfare. They wage their silly territorial battles, kill each other ruthlessly and freely, and consider themselves experts on war and suffering. But the real war has always been ahead of them, unseen, unimagined. Enemies who can't be killed by normal weapons, who have their base in an alternate universe, who are interested only in slaughtering every living being on the face of the planet."

"They know about it now," Sharmila says grimly. "They have seen the footage on television and the Internet. Hordes of soldiers firing bullets into demons, dropping bombs on them. The demons falling from the force of the bullets, shattered by the bombs. Then rising, piecing themselves back together. Coming on again. Unstoppable. Ripping the soldiers to shreds. They are still trying — or were, the last I heard — to send in more troops, to drop more destructive missiles. But they can see it is pointless. They realize now — too late — the manner of beasts they are dealing with. The human race has learned a lot about war over the past three weeks. More than I wish they ever had to."

"Have there been any nuclear retaliations?" Beranabus asks calmly.

"*Nuclear?*" Kernel and I shout at the same time.

"The politicians have resorted to nuclear assaults before," Beranabus says. "They say they don't build such bombs to use, but when the pressure builds, the fingers will come down on the buttons. Only a fool thinks otherwise."

"No nuclear strikes yet," Sharmila says. "There has been talk, and if not for the Disciples it might have happened already. But our voice has been heard at last, and officials are knocking one another over in their haste to bring us on board as advisers. We said a nuclear attack would not stop the demons, that the tunnel is of magical origin and can only be closed magically. They did not like that. Some wanted to chance a nuclear blast anyway. But for the moment they are holding off. At least they *were*. . . ."

This is crazy. We're standing here talking about nuclear bombs being dropped on Carcery Vale. It's insane.

"We have to do something!" I shout. Beranabus, Sharmila, and Kernel look at me, eyebrows raised. "We have to . . . to . . ."

Beranabus smiles cynically when I run out of words. "I wish you'd been able to finish. If you had a plan, I'd have loved to hear it. But of course you don't. I don't either. But let's hear Sharmila out and, who knows, maybe one will fall together." He turns his attention back to the Indian woman. "What have the Disciples been doing aside from advising?"

"Meera Flame led a small team in when we first realized what was happening," Sharmila says.

"*Meera*," I moan. "Is she . . . ?"

Sharmila sighs. "Most of us thought it was too soon. We did not know enough about what was going on. The general consensus was to wait a day or two, gather more information, then hit them hard. Meera rejected that plan. Dervish was her friend. She thought he might still be alive. She asked for volunteers. A few rallied to her side. They went in. Nobody has heard from them since."

"And the rest?" Beranabus asks as I reel from the news of another friend's almost certain death. "What did you do once you'd sized up the situation?"

"Not much more than Meera," Sharmila says miserably.

"We pinpointed the opening to the cave, and that was where we struck, but the demons had it guarded. Eight of our best went in, led by Shark, in the light of midday, hoping to take them by surprise. But they were ready and waiting. Two got out alive — Shark was one of them. The others . . ."

"That's bad," Beranabus grunts. "It would have been better if you'd waited for me. I know you couldn't," he says quickly as Sharmila starts to protest. "You did what would normally be the right thing. It's usually best to strike early. But as you've observed, this is a most unique attack. The demons have been marshaled by a leader who understands the ways of human warfare. Such a leader wouldn't make the mistake of leaving the cave unguarded. In this case . . ." He stops short of openly criticizing Sharmila and the other Disciples.

"It has been damage limitation since then," Sharmila says coldly, concluding her report. "We have done what we can to contain them. Ordered the grounding of all aircraft, the pulling out or destruction of boats. Established a watch to stop the demons spreading any farther. But we are fighting a losing battle. Within a couple of weeks — if it has not already happened — the exodus will begin. Once they have complete control of the country, they will move on to the next. And the next. We will defy them. Shoot down the planes and boats they commandeer, as well as those demons capable of flight. Send soldiers to stall them so we are not rushing around madly all the time. But there are already far too many for us to deal with, and more crossing every day. Unless we can stop them at the source . . ."

Sharmila falls silent. Beranabus is chewing his right thumbnail, frowning.

"We could attack from their side," Kernel suggests. "Cross universes, find the other end of the tunnel, hit them there."

"They'll be expecting that," Beranabus mumbles. "They'll have left a guard. Also, every demon within a million-world radius will be rushing to the tunnel, eager to squeeze through and get their claws on some humans before they're all gone. We wouldn't have a hope. We're too late to do anything from that side. We stop them at Carcery Vale or nowhere."

"Then Carcery Vale it is," Kernel says, and stands. "When do we go?"

"Yes," I say, taking my place beside Kernel. "When?" I expect him to say something cutting but he only looks at me calmly, then nods approvingly.

"Soon," Beranabus mutters. "We'll catch some sleep first, then —"

"*Sleep?*" I explode. "We can't waste time —"

"Let me make this as clear as I can," Beranabus cuts in. "Mankind is in its death throes. The war has come and gone. We lost. We're going to give it one last try, hit Carcery Vale with all we have, go down fighting. But go down we certainly will, bar a miracle. And while I believe in miracles, I don't think we're going to experience one this time. When we go to the Vale, we go to die. And once we're dead, the rest of humanity will soon follow.

"But we have to pretend that we *do* stand a chance. For the sake of our sanity, we must act like we believe we can pull this off. That means going in fresh and feisty, at our physical and mental best. So I'm going to sleep, fully aware that it will probably be my last-ever snooze — bar the never-ending slumber — but desperately hoping it will make the blindest bit of difference. I highly recommend that the rest of you follow suit."

With that he stumbles to the rug that serves as his bed, lies down, closes his eyes, mutters a spell, and falls asleep.

"He is right," Sharmila says softly. She looks at me and I see nothing but negativity in her eyes. "I hoped he would be able to offer hope, that he knew some secret way to stop this. But I could not believe it. We should sleep. Once we start, there might not be any later opportunities for rest."

"I'll find a blanket for you," Kernel says.

"My thanks."

While Kernel searches for a spare rug, Sharmila studies me. "What I said earlier about your uncle . . . I did not mean it. I just wanted someone to blame. I am sure it was not his fault. There are some things you cannot stop."

"No problem," I mutter, though part of me doesn't agree with her. Dervish had been hoodwinked by Juni. He was probably frantic with worry about me. His mind was elsewhere. He wouldn't have been focusing, doing his job. Maybe part of this *is* his fault — and mine — for not seeing through Juni Swan in the first place.

Kernel spreads a rug for Sharmila. She lies down as soon as it's ready and repeats Beranabus's sleeping spell. Her face goes smooth and I can tell she's having pleasant dreams.

"How about you?" Kernel asks. "Want me to teach you the spell?"

"I don't think so. It doesn't feel right, sleeping at a time like this."

Kernel shrugs. "If you don't, you'll only brood about what's happened and what lies ahead."

I think about that, then sigh wearily. "OK. Tell me." Moments later magic sends me under and I tumble gratefully into the arms of a deliberately dreamless sleep.

# VALKYRIES

✠   ✠   ✠

IN Sharmila's personal jet, streaking through the skies. I'd think that was cool any other time but I'm hard to impress right now. Versatile Sharmila is the pilot. There are six other seats. Beranabus has taken up the rear pair and is making a series of phone calls — we could have used a window to get to Carcery Vale and saved some time, but he wanted to talk with the Disciples first and maneuver them into position. Kernel is on the middle left, staring down at the clouds. I'm on the front right, flicking through newspapers.

Tales of mayhem and terror. Splash photos of demons and their victims. An array of monsters never dreamed of by most people until now. Long, sprawling lists of victims. Firsthand accounts from survivors. Speculation and theories — where are the Demonata from? What are their motives? How can we kill them?

That's the most burning question — how to destroy the invaders. Mankind has never had to face an unstoppable enemy before. There have been countless movies and books about such encounters, and the aliens or monsters have always had a weak spot, an Achilles' heel that some clean-cut champion has discovered and exploited in the nick of time. But that's not the case here. The reports are from the early days of the invasion and there's a hint of optimism in them. But even in these columns I can sense desperation as the realization seeps in — *we can't kill them!*

There are a few reports about the Disciples, but they're vague and patchy. Rumors of a group of experts with knowledge and experience of demons, but no mention of magic or names.

Some of the older papers still have ordinary sections, sports coverage, and gossip columns, the usual padding. An attempt to maintain normalcy. But the later editions focus solely on the Demonata. Nothing else, just page after page of horror and catastrophe.

I stop reading after half an hour. I've had enough. Humanity has hit a brick wall. We're facing our end, like the dinosaurs millions of years before us. The only difference is we've got journalists on hand to document every blow and setback, cataloging our rapid, painful downfall in vibrant, vicious detail. Personally, I think the dinosaurs had the better deal. When it comes to impending, unavoidable extinction, ignorance is bliss.

✠ We set down hours later on a private landing strip outside a small town close to the border where humans and demons are locked in battle. There are several other planes and helicopters parked at the sides of the strip. A large grey square building occupies one corner. We head for it once we've disembarked, Beranabus leading the way with the stride of a confident, commanding general.

Inside the building are eleven men and women, a mix of races. A couple aren't much older than me, a few look to be in their seventies or eighties, while the others fall into the thirty-to-sixty bracket. Most are neatly dressed, though one or two could compete with Beranabus in the scruffiness stakes. They all looked tired and drained.

"Hail to the chief!" a large man in military fatigues shouts ironically, saluting Beranabus as he enters. There are letters tattooed on his knuckles and a shark's head covers the flesh between knuckles and thumb. Like when Sharmila turned up at the cave, I know his face and name, even though we've never really met.

"Shark?" Beranabus scowls. "Sharmila thought you were dead."

"When you broke contact, I feared the worst," Sharmila says, shuffling around Beranabus.

"Couldn't wait for the messiah forever," Shark grunts. "There was fighting to be done. I was going to summon you back, but I knew you wouldn't return without our regal leader."

"I had to wait," Sharmila says stiffly. "Beranabus is our best hope."

Shark snorts. "*Hope?* What's that? I heard about it once, in a fairy tale."

"Be quiet," Beranabus says softly, and the larger man obeys, though he eyes Beranabus accusingly, as though he blames the magician for our dire predicament. "Any more to join us?" Beranabus asks, addressing the question to the room in general.

"Two, maybe three," a small, dark-skinned woman answers.

"Then I'll start." Beranabus looks around, meeting everybody's gaze in turn. "I won't offer false hope. We're in deep trouble, and I doubt we'll be able to wade out. But the war isn't lost yet. If we can destroy the tunnel linking the two universes, the demons will be sucked back to their own realm."

There are excited mutterings. "Are you sure?" Shark asks suspiciously. "You're not just saying that to rally our spirits?"

"Have I ever lied to any of you?" Beranabus retorts sharply. He waits a moment. When nobody responds, he continues. "One of Lord Loss's human allies killed a person in the cave in order to prime the tunnel opening. The killer later joined with the rock where the mouth of the tunnel was originally situated. He or she has become a living part of the opening. If we dismantle the tunnel walls, the killer dies, the demons get sucked back to their own universe, and all will be well with the world."

"How do we close the tunnel?" Sharmila asks.

"There's a lodestone set deep within the cave," Beranabus says. "The demons are using its power. If I can reach it, I know the spells to disable it and rid us of our unwelcome guests. I'll need somebody to help me inside the cave — Kernel or Grubbs. The rest of you only have to concern yourselves with getting us there."

"You want us to clear the way for you, even if it costs us our lives," Shark growls.

"Aye," Beranabus says. "This is a suicide mission. We're going to drop into a nest of demons. They'll be waiting for us, expecting an attack. They'll outnumber us, and many are probably more powerful than we are. Our chances of making it to the lodestone are slim. Even if the boys and I get through, the rest of you are doomed — you'll need to continue fighting while I cast the spells, to guard our backs. I doubt any of you will survive."

"That's a lot to ask," Shark says icily.

"It's no more than I ask of myself. Sacrifice opened this tunnel, and only sacrifice can close it." He glances at Kernel and me, hesitates, then pushes on. "For the spell to work, I must kill Kernel or Grubbs. If they both perish along the way, I'll offer my own life. I think I can make that work. Whatever happens, it's a death trip for me. I have to get deep inside the tunnel to work the spell. Once it's finished, I won't be able to fight my way out. I'm too old and weary."

Beranabus looks straight at Shark and awaits his response. The big man shrugs thoughtfully, and Beranabus addresses the room again. "I don't think any of us will make it through this day. But if we succeed, humanity will go on."

"Until another tunnel is opened," Sharmila notes. "If we all perish, who will protect mankind the next time?"

"That's not our problem," Beranabus says. "I believe the universe will spit out more heroes to lead the good fight. But whatever happens, it's out of our hands. This is what we must do to counter the present threat. Are you with me? If any of you aren't, say so now and leave the rest of us to get on with it."

Nobody backs down from the challenge. Most don't look very happy — who the hell would! — but they accept the magician's verdict. Seeing this, Beranabus smiles approvingly, then circulates, chatting with the Disciples individually, making sure they're prepared for the fight, offering advice and strategic tips, raising morale.

Kernel and I are in the middle of the room, looking at each other uncertainly. Beranabus's announcement that one of us must be sacrificed came out of the blue. Neither of us knows what to say. It's one thing to go into a fight knowing you'll probably lose. Quite another to be told that to win, you must offer up your throat to be slit.

Sharmila approaches, smiling thinly. "He did not tell you that you were to be killed?"

"He's a busy man," Kernel snaps. "He doesn't have time to tell us everything."

Sharmila sighs. "You are loyal. That is good. But are you loyal to the point of death? Will you allow yourself to be slaughtered?" She looks at me. "Will *you*?"

"We'll do what we must," Kernel says fiercely. "We're not ignorant children. We know our duty. If we have to die, so be it. We'd rather not, but we'll be killed by the demons anyway if we lose, and probably more painfully and slowly."

Sharmila tilts her head toward us. "I apologize if I seemed critical. But I had to know the nature of the boys I am to fight and die for. Now I am confident that you will not fail if the opportunity presents itself. Thank you for reassuring me."

She wanders off to talk with Beranabus. Kernel looks sideways at me. "I normally wouldn't give another person's word for them, especially when I'm not sure of it, but it seemed like the right thing to say."

"You don't have to worry about me," I reply stiffly. "I won't let us down."

"I wish I could believe that." He doesn't say it to hurt me. Just speaking the truth as he sees it.

"I chickened out in the Demonata's universe," I whisper, blushing. "But this is different. I'll fight. And I'll die if I have to. I'm not afraid of dying, no more than anybody else in this room."

"Really?" Kernel's unconvinced. "If I fall, and you and Beranabus make it to the lodestone, you'll let him drive a knife through your heart or chop off your head?"

"Without a moment's hesitation. Not because I'm incredibly brave, but because I'm terribly afraid." I give a sickly laugh. "If I don't let him kill me, it would mean fighting to survive in a world overrun by demons. The thought of that scares me more than death."

Kernel chuckles. "Know something crazy? I believe you." He offers his hand and I take it. "Good luck, Grubbs."

"Good luck."

"May we both die honorably," he says.

"And take every damn demon down with us," I add with a twisted grin.

✠ Tooling up. Everybody arms themselves with guns, knives, axes — pretty much anything we can carry. Demons can't be killed by regular weapons, but we can invest the blades and bullets with magical powers.

"How many of the Disciples are capable of killing demons?" I ask Kernel, testing short swords for feel and weight.

"In this universe?" He pulls a face. "If it was a normal crossing . . . Sharmila, Shark, one or two others. But there's more energy in the air because it's a tunnel, not a window.

Others should be able to tap into that and find the ability to kill. If we're lucky."

One more Disciple arrives while we're getting ready. An ancient, tiny woman who walks with the aid of a cane. The sight of her picking up a mace and swinging it over her head makes me smile. A few of the others grin too. But then she mutters a quick spell and a crop of seven-inch-long blades grow out of the mace head, which glows with magical energy. Nobody doubts her after that.

Then it's to the helicopters that Shark has arranged through his contacts in various armies. We're going to fly in and set down as close to the cave entrance as we can. Three helicopters, five of us to each. I'm with Beranabus, Kernel, Shark, and Sharmila — the core of the force. Our pilot's an ordinary human, as are the other two. Soldiers on loan from the forces currently engaged in hopeless warfare with the Demonata. Shark has told a few commanders of our plan. They've handed him control of their troops and will do whatever else they can to assist.

The helicopter rises smoothly, as if the ground is dropping away. I haven't been in a helicopter before. It's a curious sensation. Not as much of a blast as flying through the sky with Beranabus, but way more interesting than a plane.

"I never thought I'd be doing this," Shark bellows over the noise of the whirring blades. He's smiling. "How often does the chance come along to end a war? You see it all the time in films, but in real life wars are decided over a variety of fronts and battles. It's possible to play an important role in victory, but only a limited part. To actually be charged with the task of going in and saving the world . . ." He whoops with joy.

"I'm glad you're having fun," Kernel remarks sarcastically.

"Damn straight I am," he hollers. "Might as well — we're going to die regardless."

I turn my attention away from the battle-hungry Shark. He's probably got the right attitude for a fight like this, but I find his gung-ho approach tasteless and disturbing. This isn't a game. We're not competing for a trophy. If we lose, we take humanity down with us. I don't see how you can be anything but stone-cold miserable when burdened with a responsibility like that.

Looking down as we whiz along, closing in on Carcery Vale. We're deep into Demonata territory now. This used to be my home. Not anymore. It's theirs now. Abandoned cars. Burning buildings. Pools of blood smear the roads and fields. Slaughtered animals and humans everywhere, some cut up into bits and strewn about the place, others arranged in obscene patterns by the demons, either for their own amusement or to scare anyone who ventures into their realm.

I spot a few of the monsters messing with bodies on the ground. I don't look closely enough to determine whether their victims are alive or dead. I turn my gaze away and pray for their sakes that they're corpses.

Others are lounging in trees or in patches of shade, sheltering from the sun. Although stronger demons can move about during the day, they don't like sunlight and aren't as powerful as they are at night. The land would be teeming with lots more of the beasts if we were a few hours later in the day.

The outskirts of Carcery Vale. More of a visible demonic presence. Most of the buildings are ripped to pieces. Bodies scattered everywhere. We fly over my old school — dozens of children and teachers are impaled on spikes, grey and red, covered in feasting flies, slowly rotting.

For the first time I think about my friends. Until now I've been fixed on Dervish and Bill-E. But all the others will have fallen to the Demonata too. Frank, Mary, Leon, Shannon . . . *Reni*. I rip my gaze away from the bodies in case I spot the face of someone I know. Tears come but I fight them back. I can't think about my friends, not even my uncle and brother. The best — only — way I can avenge them is by focusing on the demons and the battle. No room for pity, doubt, or fear. Mustn't imagine them suffering, the pain they must have gone through, whether any escaped. The demons. The cave. Dying. These should be my only concerns.

The air above the Vale is thick with planes and helicopters. Shark ordered the regular troops in ahead of us. They've been blanket-bombing the area for the past twenty minutes, most of their force aimed at the demons around the entrance to the cave, disrupting them, blowing up the bodies of the lesser demons. The effects are temporary — the demons will piece themselves back together once the shelling stops — but any minor advantage is a bonus.

Zoning in on the cave. I don't recognize the area anymore. There used to be a forest here at the back of our house, stretching all the way to Carcery Vale and for many miles in other directions. Now it's been firebombed into oblivion. The land is ash and tree stumps. Bare, scarred, dead. It resembles the face of an asteroid. Doesn't belong to this world. Something from outer space or a bad dream.

We fly over the rubbly ruins of a large building. We're several seconds past it before I realize — that wreck used to be my home! The wonderful three-story mansion has been reduced to a skeletal shell. I'm almost glad Dervish isn't here to see it. He loved that house. The sight of it in this sorry state would bring tears to his eyes.

The pilot's in constant contact with the other aircraft, snapping orders and directions, carefully maneuvering his way through the fleet. If he's scared, he doesn't show it. I wish the fighting could be left to the professionals like him. But I guess ordinary people always get sucked into battles. It's the nature of warfare.

"Like a scene out of hell, isn't it?" Shark notes with relish, stroking the long, gleaming barrel of a machine gun hanging from his neck.

"Let us hope it is hell for the demons when we finish," Sharmila says.

The helicopter stops advancing. Hovers in the air, the pilot waiting for the other two copters to join us. I stare at the ground. Hard to spot the cave entrance. Bombs are going off all around, throwing up dirt, stones, bits of flesh, and bones. I see stronger demons moving about freely, protected from the explosions by magic. They form a large circle, several demons deep. Pinpointing the center of that circle, I finally locate the mouth of the cave. Just a small hole in the ground. Doesn't look like anything special. Not the sort of place where you expect the future of the planet to be decided.

The second helicopter moves up alongside us, then the third. The Disciples are on their feet or knees by the open sides of the copters, clinging to straps, ready to jump as soon as they're within safe distance of the ground. The elderly woman with the cane is sitting, legs dangling over the side, stroking the blades sticking out of her mace.

Our pilot looks back at Shark for confirmation. The ex-soldier pauses and casts an unusually sad eye around, swallowing hard, looking doubtful for the first time. For a moment I think he's lost his thirst for battle. Beranabus thinks it too and opens his mouth to yell an order at the pilot. Then Shark raises his head, grins grimly, and nods savagely. The pilot speaks rapidly into his mouthpiece, issuing urgent orders. The sky clears of planes. Helicopters packed with ground troops cluster around us. I can see the faces of some of the soldiers — underlying terror, overlaid by determination, much like the faces of those closer to me.

The rain of bombs lessens, then stops. Dust swirls below, momentarily masking the hordes of demons. Shark roars commandingly at the pilot.

We drop.

# SPARTANS

✠   ✠   ✠

THE demons attack before we touch the ground, screaming hatefully, hurling themselves at us viciously. More pour out of the cave entrance, all manner of foul monsters, multi-limbed, fangs the size of scythes, claws galore, spitting venom, breathing fire — the works!

The soldiers bear the brunt of the assault. They spill out of the helicopters and absorb the rush of demons, firing off round after round of bullets that they know will only delay the beasts, buying precious seconds for those of us in the three central helicopters, laying down their lives to help us.

As the bloodshed begins, Beranabus claps me hard on the back. Almost before I know what's happening, I'm out of the helicopter and running, Beranabus slightly ahead of me, Kernel to my right, Shark and Sharmila flanking us. The other ten Disciples fan out. Everyone's focused on protecting Beranabus, Kernel, and me. Even Shark, who'd love to mindlessly lay into the demons, sticks close by, acting only when we come under direct threat.

For several seconds we glide through the ranks of Demonata as if they weren't there. A few challenge us, but the Disciples brush them off without slowing, sending them tumbling out of our way, interested only in clearing a path to the cave. The demons are hell-bent on butchering the soldiers — easy targets for the magical monsters — delighted to have so many new victims drop in on them at once.

Then a familiar demon master rises into the air above the cave entrance. My hands clench into fists, nails breaking the flesh of my palms, and the hope that had been forming within me quickly dwindles away.

It's Lord Loss.

"Demonata!" my old enemy cries, the word piercing my skull and those of everyone and everything around me. "Beware the Disciples! Block their path or we'll be returned to our own universe!"

In an instant the battle changes. Every demon shrugs off the attentions of the soldiers and focuses on our small band. Impossible to tell how many there are . . . a couple hundred or more. As if breathing in unison, they all snarl at once, then converge.

A wave of demons breaks over us sickeningly fast. One moment they're yards away. The next we're surrounded. Claws flash, jaws snap, at least a dozen demons to each of us. Three Disciples perish immediately, wrestled to the ground, ripped to pieces. The rest are stranded, cut off from one another, reduced to fighting isolated, individual battles.

Shark disappears beneath three lumpy monsters, then reappears a second later, throwing them off with a ball of magical energy, laughing maniacally.

Sharmila is muttering spells frantically, gently touching the demons around her, setting them on fire.

The woman with the cane is using it like a gun, shooting bursts of magical bullets at the demons, crushing the heads of others with her mace.

Beranabus presses on, ignoring the carnage, intent on making it to the cave. Kernel runs behind him. So do I, legs working automatically, leaping over the struggling demons, Disciples, and soldiers, panting hard. I want to flee. The coward inside me wails and pleads with me to retreat. But I think of Dervish and Bill-E and cling to the belief that they're alive, that I can save them. That gives me the strength to ignore the craven cries and follow Beranabus and Kernel.

A rabbit-shaped demon leaps up in front of Beranabus. I recognize it from the massacre on the plane. It's Femur, one of Lord Loss's familiars. It vomits acid at Beranabus's face. But the magician is prepared and deflects the acid back at Femur. It drenches the demon and eats through its fur and skin. Femur screams and rolls away, tiny paws frantically trying to wipe the burning liquid away from its cheeks and eyes before its head melts down to the bone.

The hell child known as Artery appears, grabs Beranabus's left leg with his mouth-encrusted hands, and bites hard. Beranabus grunts, then kicks Artery as if he were a football, sending him flying over the heads of several other demons.

Beranabus staggers on. The cave entrance is within sight. So is Lord Loss, still hovering in the air, all eight arms extended, smiling sorrowfully.

A tiger-headed demon latches onto my waist and whirls me around, fangs snapping in search of my throat. The magic within me instinctively sends a wave of electricity through the monster. It turns black, then collapses, synapses sizzling, eyes melting in its sockets.

"Nice work!" Shark yells, appearing beside me. He's bleeding from several cuts, and one of his ears has been bitten off. "Came to help, but it looks like you don't need me."

"Beranabus!" I shout at him. "You have to help Ber —"

Before I can finish, Shark's gone, ripped away by a gaggle of demons who swarm over him, antlike. I see a hand . . . his teeth as he bites . . . I hear a laugh . . . then he's on the ground, covered completely, and I see nothing more of him.

I take a stunned step away from where Shark fell and look around, dazed, searching for Beranabus. He's come to a standstill. A dozen or more demons stand between the magician and the hole. He fires magical bolts at them, but they take his best shots, barely blink, then return fire. There's no way around. Soon they'll wear him down and move in to finish him off.

Kernel slides to his master's side and joins the fight. But just as he fires off a few pinkish bolts of his own, the scorpion demon from the plane — Spine — leaps onto his bald brown head and aims its stinger at his right eye. With a pop the stinger goes in, then comes out wet and glistening. Shrieking with delight, the demon spits out a mouthful of eggs, filling Kernel's pulpy socket.

Kernel screams with agony as the eggs hatch and maggoty insects gnaw at what's left of his eye, before working their way through to his brain. He wheels away from Beranabus, losing all sense of direction. Spine strikes again and Kernel's left eye pops too.

Something hits me hard in my upper back and I slam to the ground. Claws dig into my flesh. I'm momentarily stunned, unable to use my magic. I feel the end coming and a large part of me welcomes it — anything to break clear of this madness. But then the demon's thrown from me by a blast of magical power. I sit up, groggy, expecting to find Sharmila or the lady with the cane. But neither woman is anywhere to be seen. I can only see demons and Beranabus struggling against them desperately, hopelessly. Then who . . . ?

"Nobody touches the boy!" Lord Loss bellows, and I realize I've been rescued by the demon master. He catches my eye and his smile broadens. "I'm saving you for myself, Grubitsch. You escaped on the airplane, but you will not wriggle free again."

The fighting clears around me, demons giving me a wide berth, turning aside to finish off the Disciples and the few remaining soldiers. The path to the hole clears — but it's also the path to Lord Loss. For a long second I stare at the demon master, hovering, waiting. I want to run away. No point trying to push on — Lord Loss will kill me before I get anywhere near the cave. The wise thing would be to turn tail and —

"No!" I yell, deciding not to be a coward, to die with everyone else if that's my destiny, to perish slowly and awfully at the hands of Lord Loss if that's the cost of failure. But I'm not going to flee. I'm through running. It's time to fight.

I lurch ahead, summoning all my reserves of energy, speaking quickly to the magic within me, saying I know I've let it down in the past and held it back, but promising it a free rein now. We're in this together, and I won't stop until I'm dead or we've won. Will it help me?

The magic screams back its answer — *Hell, yes!* — and I feel power grow in the pit of my stomach, greater than any I've unleashed before. I don't know if I'll prove a match for Lord Loss and his companions, but right now I feel like I can't be beaten, like I'm the most powerful player here.

"Beranabus!" I shout, almost at the hole, risking a look back. He's surrounded by demons. Cursing, I aim a hand at them and let loose the magic. White flames leap from the tips of my fingers. They hit the demons hard and fire streaks through them like lightning. The demons shriek and peel aside, covered by flames they can't quench, some coming apart at the seams and dying instantly.

"Balor's eye!" Beranabus grunts, limping toward me, stooping to pick up the screaming and writhing Kernel, dragging him along. "I knew you were powerful, but not *that* powerful!"

"Oh, yes," Lord Loss says overhead. "Grubitsch is a most remarkable boy. That is why I chose not to fight him in the cave when I first had the opportunity to kill him. I did not care to face him alone in a place of magic."

"You were afraid!" I holler, reaching the mouth of the cave, sneering up at Lord Loss, feeling invincible. For the first time I believe we can do this — we can win!

"Afraid?" Lord Loss murmurs. "An ugly word, Grubitsch. And not entirely accurate. I was not afraid to fight you. I merely preferred to do so when the odds were stacked in my favor. After all, why fight by yourself when you can wait for . . . ?" He smiles wickedly and gestures to the hole.

I look down and my sense of triumph fizzles out like a live match that's been dunked in a bucket of water.

The tunnel leading down to the cave is full of demons. And I mean *full*. There are more of the creatures down there than up here. Thousands of evil eyes glint at me. An army of jaws open hungrily to reveal row after row of sharpened teeth. And in the claws of the beast closest to me — Dervish's severed, lifeless, blood-rimmed head! Another demon holds the hacked-off head of Reni Gossel. Frank Martin. Charlie Rall. Meera Flame. All the people I cared about. Bill-E's the only one missing — or maybe he's farther back, where I can't see him.

"I made your friends and family my first priority," Lord Loss says proudly as my world burns at the edges and madness swooshes down upon me. "I told you I would punish you for humiliating me. A dreadful, all-encompassing punishment. This is how I respond to mockery, Grubitsch. Look upon my work and know at last the true, heartless wrath of Lord Loss."

"Grubbs!" Beranabus shouts. "They don't matter! Ignore them! We —"

"Do not disturb the boy," Lord Loss interrupts gloomily. "This is a time for true grief, not false promise and meaningless heroics. Look down, Beranabus. Even an eternal dreamer like you can't believe in hope now. It's over. The war has been decided. Mankind has fallen."

"Grubbs! We can still . . ."

The rest of Beranabus's words are lost to me. Lord Loss is right. We're finished. There's no way through. Everyone I knew — dead. Everyone I know who hasn't already fallen to the Demonata — soon to be dead. And everybody else, the billions of men, women, and children spread across the world, whom I never would have known, even if I'd lived a thousand lifetimes — they'll all die too.

I sink to my knees, the enormity of the moment over-whelming me. Beranabus grabs my right shoulder with one hand — still holding the wailing, thrashing Kernel with the other — and tries jerking me back to my feet. But I stay where I am, tears flowing, dread consuming me, hoping Lord Loss doesn't drag the torment out too long, praying for him to take pity on me and kill me quickly.

I rock back and forth, moaning, glancing around, seeing demons in the throes of celebration, corpses of soldiers and Disciples being passed around like appetizers at a party. Their howls, grunts, and chattering start to sound like music to my ears or the chanting of a long, complicated spell. Then I realize — the sound isn't of demonic origin. It's coming from somewhere else . . . from the rocks beneath me.

I look down, expecting some new torment of Lord Loss's. Instead, I find the face of the girl — Bec — bulging out of the rock, eyes open, lips moving swiftly. Beranabus sees it too. His fingers go limp on my shoulder as he stares at the face, lost for words, forgetting all about the demons and our fool-ish quest.

"What's this?" Lord Loss frowns. "Little Bec, present and alert after all these centuries? Impossible. How can her soul have . . . ?" He smiles. "No matter. She is powerful, Beranabus, even more than you or Grubitsch. But she cannot save you. Trapped in the rocks, she can only mourn your sad passing."

The girl speaks faster than ever, her lips a blur. I feel the magic inside me pulse in time with her chanting. I can't understand her, but the magic does, and it swirls around inside me, excited, trying to reach out to her. Since I've nothing to lose, I let it have its way. I step back mentally and let the magic and the girl communicate freely. As the pair link in some unknowable way, I feel my own lips moving, the girl's words becoming mine, like when I was relaying her previous outburst to Beranabus in his cave.

"Come now," Lord Loss says, descending gracefully, signaling to the demons around us. "Enough of this childishness. Surrender, Grubitsch, and I will go easy on you. Well . . . easier than I planned to."

"We'll never surrender!" Beranabus roars, coming alive again, releasing me and Kernel, bringing up his hands to engage the demon master in battle.

"Take him," Lord Loss says, yawning mockingly. The nearest demons howl and hurl themselves at the magician — then strike against an invisible boundary and bounce back off it.

"Impressive," Lord Loss murmurs. "But how long do you think you can sustain such a barrier, old man?"

"This isn't my work," Beranabus says, staring at me uncertainly. The girl's hands have formed now and stick stiffly out of the ground, grey and rocky. I take them, my fingers large and chunky in comparison to hers. We continue to babble, her, me, and the magic.

Kernel screams as maggots chew their way deeper into his brain. He jerks aside wildly and the demons eagerly grab for him, but he rebounds against the barrier and is hurled to the ground, landing by my knees. Beranabus stoops and puts his fingers to the boy's forehead. Magic flares. Maggots fall out of Kernel's bleeding sockets and shrivel, dead before they hit the ground. Kernel moans and slumps unconscious.

Beranabus faces me, features alive with hope. "Let's go!" He grasps my elbow. "If you can maintain this barrier, they can't stop from us from getting into the cave. We —"

My head whips toward him and the girl barks something, using my lips. I don't know what she says, but it brings a groan of desperation from Beranabus. "No! You can't tell me that. Not now. Not after all this. Not when we're so close."

I've no time to ponder his words. My eyes refocus on the girl's and lock on her peculiar stony pupils. We're speaking faster, louder, a fierce magical energy building around us, causing all the hairs on my body to stand up, then burn down to their roots. My clothes also burn away. So do Beranabus's and Kernel's. Within seconds we're naked and hairless, and still the energy builds.

Lord Loss senses danger. "Get them!" he bellows. "Destroy that barrier! Kill them all!"

The demons scurry to obey, but their efforts are wasted. The barrier repels them casually. The harder they throw themselves against it, the harder they rebound. Bolts of magic are returned magnified, tearing apart those who fired them. They try to claw it to pieces, rip it apart with their teeth, burrow underneath to attack from within the earth, all to no avail.

The energy is unbearable. It goes beyond all my notions of normal heat. I think this is what it would be like to hover within the heart of the sun. The rock is melting around the girl's face, but she remains, more of her form becoming visible as the stone recedes.

Screams of panic. With an effort I raise my head. The demons are staring at the sky, horrified and bewildered. Looking up, I see something incomprehensible. The sky is *pulsing*. It's like looking at the underside of a trampoline while somebody leaps up and down on top. In the center, a funnel has formed, as if the universe is being pulled toward one point. As I watch, it throbs low, then pulls up high . . . low-high . . . low-high. And it might be my imagination, but it seems as if the tip of the funnel hangs directly over me, Kernel, Beranabus, and the ghost girl, Bec.

Lights flicker across the distorted sky. Clouds burst into flame. The tip of the funnel pushes lower and lower, ever closer to us. The demons scatter, screeching and keening. Stuff like this happens every day in their own universe. They aren't bothered by magical madness there. But they didn't expect it in this universe of order and sanity. They don't know what it means or how to respond.

"This will not save you!" Lord Loss shouts none too convincingly. "Stay, you scum!" he roars at the fleeing demons. "Fight! We can break through this barrier and kill them. You must not . . ."

I tune him out. My lips are my own again during a brief pause in the spell. "What's happening?" I wheeze, directing the question at Beranabus. But he can only shake his head and stare at Bec and me. Then the spell starts again and I can't ask any more questions. My lips are Bec's. My magic and her magic — one. Our minds join. I get flashes of her life —

a simple farming society, demons, a quest, warriors, a magician, closing the tunnel between worlds, sacrificing herself, trapped in a cave, her spirit somehow separating from her body, dying but not moving on, imprisoned, no way out, haunting the centuries, unable to escape the rocky confines of the cave.

Then I'm inside somebody else's head. I see a small, modern village, thousands of patches of light in the sky around me, a baby who looks oddly familiar, a young punk who . . . no, surely that's not Dervish! Yes, it is, a young and spiky-haired Dervish Grady, fighting alongside Shark, Sharmila, Beranabus, a dark-skinned man, and . . .

Kernel sits up and groans. He shakes his head groggily. His empty sockets turn left and right as if he's looking for something. They fix sightlessly on Bec and me. Trembling, moaning with pain, he reaches over and lays his hands on top of mine. My magic shoots out to him, then blasts back stronger than ever, drawing power from the blind teenager. His lips move along with mine and Bec's, his magic mingling with ours.

Our voices rise. The sky turns black, red, white. Rocks are ripping out of the ground, shooting upward, burning, turning into birds, cows, cars, people, then back into rocks. Now everything's rising, the ruins of trees and buildings, corpses, the demons. Gravity loses its grip. Lord Loss tries clinging to the invisible barrier around us but is ripped away and up. He hurls vile curses at us as he shoots off.

The world is coming apart. Everything's being destroyed. I'm afraid now, even more than when I thought the demons had us. Bec must be insane. Sixteen hundred years of captivity have driven her mad. She only wants to ruin, make everybody else suffer as she has suffered, tear the world apart. And she can do it. With my magic and Kernel's, she has the power to wreak a terrible, misdirected revenge.

I try stopping it. I focus on breaking contact, making my lips stop, getting out of here before all is lost. But the magic holds me tight. There's no escaping. Everything in sight shoots skyward, while the sky itself drops ever farther, the tip of the funnel pulsing down . . . down . . . down.

Beranabus is frightened too. He was exhilarated when he saw the demons get swept away, but this has exploded out of control. He sees what I see — the literal end of the world. He sits on the ground — the only patch left is the bit contained by our bubble of energy — and gapes at the three of us, eyes wide, twin pools of confusion and fear. Maybe he thinks about killing one of us to stop it. But I don't think he could. He doesn't have the power.

The tip of the funnel is almost upon us. I gear myself up for one last effort, one final push to break the unnatural, destructive bond between me, Kernel, and Bec. But before I can attempt anything, the tip of the funnel — blue, like the sky used to be — touches the wall of the invisible boundary.

A flash of light that is every color. My body explodes, or seems to. I have the feeling of being everywhere and nowhere at once, both an entire universe and an insignificant speck. The funnel sucks me into it. Millions of panels of pulsing lights. Flying from one to another, bouncing around, moving so fast I'm creating a vacuum, sucking the tip of the funnel in after me, pulling it along in my wake. Dimly aware of Kernel and Bec's magic working in tandem with mine.

We stop bouncing but move quicker than ever. A cluster of purple lights flash, then bolt together and become a small window. We shoot through it. Yellow lights flash and join — we fly through. A series of flashing lights and windows, one after the other, faster and faster. Curious, I focus on the magic and realize Kernel's the one creating the windows and directing us through them. I've no idea how or why. I don't think Kernel knows either.

No sense of time or space. Just one window after another, the colors whirring and blurring, a fearsome noise building in the background. Then the lights fade. Unable to see anything now. Total blackness. As blind as Kernel.

The noise continues to build, so loud it could crush a continent. My ears burst. My skull cracks. My brain bubbles away to nothing. But that makes no difference. I still exist. I still hear, think, and feel. The noise squeezes my soul. Pain that's indescribable. No way to scream or release the pressure. A universe of agony.

Then, suddenly, the noise stops. I come to rest. The pain disappears. Delicious, soothing silence. Broken abruptly by a girl's delighted laugh.

# A SECOND CHANCE

✠　　✠　　✠

At first I think the world and universe have been utterly destroyed and I'm just imagining the laughter. But then the blackness clears slightly. I realize I have eyes again. Blinking, I look around but can't make out much. It's night and I'm in the middle of a cluster of trees. It's not especially dark — the gleam of a full moon seeps through the branches of the trees — but it's hard to adjust or focus. My mind's spinning crazily in a bewildered whir.

"What happened?" Beranabus croaks, rising from a spot nearby. Kernel lies at the magician's feet, groaning, cradling his head in his hands. "Where are we?"

"I don't know," I whisper. My ears are searching for something. I'm not sure what it is, until after a few seconds it sinks in — the girl's voice has gone.

Kernel mutters something, then bolts upright, screaming. "My eyes!" he howls. "The maggots! My eyes! I can't —"

Beranabus covers his assistant's mouth and whispers words of magic, a spell to ease the pain. Kernel thrashes wildly, then regains control and stops struggling, though his chest continues to rise and fall rapidly.

Beranabus removes his hand. "Are you going to be all right?"

"My eyes . . . ?" Kernel moans.

"Gone," Beranabus says bluntly.

"But . . . we must . . . there has to be some way . . ."

"No. They're ruined. But don't worry — magic will compensate. You won't be entirely helpless." Beranabus squeezes the back of Kernel's neck. "We might even be able to knock together a pair of replacements when we return to the demon universe. If the gods are truly with us, you'll still be able to see the patches of light and create windows."

"Like I give a damn about that!" Kernel snaps sourly, but Beranabus ignores the hostility.

"Peace for a few minutes," the magician says. "I need to determine where we are."

He turns in a slow circle, eyes closed, breathing softly, trying to pinpoint our position. I know I should keep silent and wait for him to finish, but I can't. "What did she do to us? The ground breaking apart and rising . . . the sky and funnel . . . the lights and windows . . . the noise and pain. What was all that about?"

"How should I know?" Beranabus growls. "Maybe she was trying to destroy the demons and the spell got out of hand."

"But the sky! Did you see it? How did she do that? What —"

"Quiet!" Beranabus barks, opening an eye to glare at me. "How can I concentrate with you throwing stupid questions at me?"

"But she tore up the ground!" I shout. "She reversed gravity and brought the sky crashing down. And then she sent us . . . where? Is this Earth? A demon world? Are we dead?"

"I don't know." Beranabus sighs. "I don't know where this is or how she sent us here — teleportation, I suppose, but I've never seen it done that way before. But I know *why* she did it." He hesitates, then opens the other eye and looks at me with a shamed grimace. "I made another mistake. There have been far too many lately. I missed the sacrifice being made in the cave. I was wrong about Lord Loss not wanting to reopen the tunnel. And now I know my plan to close it was flawed.

"I told the Disciples that if we collapsed the walls of the tunnel, victory would be ours. The demons would be sucked back to their own universe. That's how it's happened in the past. I assumed the rules would apply the same way in the present.

"Bec told me they wouldn't."

"You mean, even if we'd succeeded, we wouldn't have gotten rid of the demons?" I ask quietly.

"We'd have stopped others from crossing," he says. "And those here would have lost much of their power. But the world has changed. There's less magic in the air. My spells wouldn't have dislodged the demons. The masters would have remained, and even weakened they would have had enough strength to crush humanity. I don't think all of the Demonata were aware of that — they certainly didn't act like they were — but Bec knew we were doomed. To spare us, she worked a spell with you and Kernel to get us out, so we could regroup and try again."

"What's there to try?" I sob. "If we couldn't send them back this time, with all the Disciples to back us up . . . if destroying the tunnel won't work . . ."

"There must be a way," Beranabus mutters. "That's why I have to focus. Time's precious. Bec gave the demons a taste of their own hellish magic, but there's no guarantee that those sucked up into the sky are dead. Even if they are, the tunnel's still open. More can cross. We need to return and block their way. So be quiet and let me get my bearings. You can ask all the questions you want after that."

He closes his eyes and turns again, reaching out with all his senses. Kernel has dragged himself away to sit against a tree. He's exploring the empty sockets of his eyes with trembling fingers, picking out some dead maggots caught in the corners. I hobble over to check on him, to help if I can, to comfort him if he'll let me.

Then I see the rocks.

My eyes have adjusted and the light from the moon is strong, even under the cover of the trees. I can't miss the rocks. They lie scattered everywhere, but a lot are piled up on my left in a large mound. They can't be real. It isn't possible. I must be imagining them. Except I'm not. The magic inside me says they're genuine. It's smug. Confident. Triumphant.

"Beranabus."

"Grubbs!" he yells angrily. "I told you not to —"

"I know where we are."

He opens his eyes a fraction, suspiciously. "Where?"

"You don't need magic. Just look." I point to the rocks.

Beranabus frowns. Then he realizes he's seen the mound before and his jaw drops. "No," he croaks. "It can't be. This is a trick. Or somewhere that looks like . . ."

"No." I walk across, pick up one of the smaller rocks, then lob it down the hole on the other side of the mound — the mouth of an all too familiar cave. "We haven't gone anywhere. We're still in Carcery Vale."

�֍ Beranabus is striding around the hole, squinting at it, studying it from every possible angle. Every so often he stops, mumbles to himself, shuffles toward the hole, then starts marching again.

I'm with Kernel. I've wiped away the worst of the muck from around his eyes, using leaves and forest water. "How are you feeling?" I ask.

"There's not much pain," he says, "but there will be. You can delay it in circumstances like these, but not indefinitely. I'll need hospital treatment when the spell wears off. Assuming any hospitals are left . . ." His head turns left, then right. "Is it day or night?"

"Night."

"I thought so. But it was day when we attacked. I didn't think I'd been unconscious that long."

"You weren't."

"Then . . . ?" He leaves the question hanging.

"We don't know," I tell him. "Beranabus is trying to figure it out."

Kernel nods slowly. "How do I look?" he asks.

I stare into the vacant pits where his eyes once were.

They're peppered with dead maggots. A few are only half visible, their heads and upper bodies buried in the dark flesh and bone of his sockets. "Fine," I lie.

Beranabus begins to laugh. I think he's laughing at my lie and I turn on him angrily. But then I see that he didn't even hear what I said.

"Of course," he chortles. "It's the only answer. There's just one way she could have channeled that much power, to such an effect. You and Bec are the other two pieces. That's the only thing that makes . . ."

He mumbles his way back into silence. I say nothing, waiting for him to get it clear in his head, so he can explain it to me in simple terms. I study him while I'm waiting. He looks weird minus his beard and hair, naked as the day he was born. I guess I look pretty strange too, as bare and hairless as an egg. I'd feel awkward any other time, but things have been so crazy in the past hour I'm not bothered by my ultrasmooth nudity.

Beranabus glances up and waves a hand at the trees. Their branches part, granting him an unobstructed view of the moon and surrounding sky. His eyes dart from the moon to the stars. I can practically hear his brain whirring as he performs silent calculations. Then the branches rustle back together and he laughs again. "I knew it!"

Beranabus bounds over to where Kernel and I are waiting. He crouches beside us, beaming like a proud father whose wife has just given birth. "The prime rule of magic — anything is possible. It's the first thing I teach my assistants, but when you've been doing it as long as I have, it's easy to forget your own advice. Just because something hasn't been done before, and just because the power involved is way beyond that of even the greatest demon master, doesn't mean it *can't* be done. Bec must have realized what she really was. She spent centuries preparing herself, waiting patiently . . .

"Or maybe she only saw how to do it during the battle. Maybe you were the catalyst, Grubbs. Or Kernel. Though I don't think so — he came last to the union, didn't he? I don't suppose it really matters. Maybe Bec can tell us, assuming she's . . ." He stops. "Yes, she must be alive — I mean, her ghost must still be here. It has to be. At least, I suppose . . ." He trails off into silence again.

"In your own time, Beranabus," I mutter impatiently. "Whenever you're ready."

He flashes me a crazy smile. "This is so extraordinary. Every time I think about it, I discover something new. We've taken an immense leap forward — well, a leap backward if you want to be pedantic. It's like going from the first stone wheel to the first manned flight in the space of one incredible day, one amazing spell. This requires years of study and analysis. We have to figure out how the three of you did it, how to control the power, what else we can do. That will —"

"I'm going to hit you if you don't stop babbling," I warn him. "Tell us what you know — or what you guess," I add quickly as he opens his mouth to start telling me he doesn't know anything really.

"I know you're in the dark, I know you want answers, just as much as I do. But . . ." He stops, focuses, takes a deep breath. "You asked me a question once, Kernel. It's a question most

Disciples have asked, normally not long after I've told them that with magic anything is possible. Can you remember what it was?"

"I'm in no mood to solve puzzles," Kernel sighs. "I just want my eyes back. Can you do that for me?"

"Not now," Beranabus huffs, waving the question away. "Think, boy. You were telling me about your early life, the night you created your first window and stepped into the universe of the Demonata. You said all your troubles started then, that if you could go back and stop yourself, everything would be fine. You asked me if —"

"No!" Kernel grunts. "It can't be."

"That's what I thought at first," Beranabus chuckles.

"But you said we couldn't!" Kernel protests.

"And I was right. Nobody ever had, and I didn't think anyone could. But now we have. You, Bec, and Grubbs did it. You broke the final barrier. I never thought it could happen. I gave up on the notion long, long ago. When you've seen as much of —"

"What is it?" I cut in sharply, furious with ignorance. "What's the big secret? What question did Kernel ask?"

"The one they all ask eventually," Beranabus smiles. "The one you would have put to me if you'd been with me a little longer, when you looked back on all the times you went wrong, wondered how things would have turned out if you'd done this or that differently, gone down one path instead of another."

Beranabus stops, glances up at the trees and the moon beyond, as if to reconfirm it before saying it out loud. When he looks at me again, the smile's still there, but shaky, as if he's not sure whether he should be smiling or not. And he says, very softly, "Kernel asked me if it was possible to travel back in time."

✠ A shocked moment of incredulous silence. Then I laugh. "Good one. You almost had me going. Now quit with the jokes and —"

"This isn't a joke," Beranabus says.

"You're trying to tell me we've returned to the past, like in some bad sci-fi movie?"

"No." Kernel giggles, then hits me with the punch line. "Like in some *very good* sci-fi movie."

"Don't," I mutter. "Things are crazy enough without you two veering off on some ludicrous tangent. We need to think about this logically, go through what happened step by step, so we can understand. Wild speculation won't get us anywhere."

"It's not wild," Beranabus says. "And it's not speculation. It's fact."

"I don't accept that. You're wrong."

"How else can you explain this?" He points to the hole, the rocks, the trees.

"It's an illusion. Our minds have conjured it up, or Bec fed the image to us to spare us the real, grisly truth. It happened to me before, in Slawter. Maybe we're lying by the cave entrance, unconscious, demons ravaging our bodies, and this is our only way out of the pain. Or we've gone into the universe of the Demonata and created this scene ourselves. Hell, maybe we're dead and this is what we've chosen for the afterlife."

"We're not dead," Kernel says. "And we're not imagining this. I'd have given myself eyes if we were."

"Time travel's impossible," I say slowly, as if explaining something obvious to a young child.

"So is flying," Beranabus says, "but you've soared like a bird."

"That's different," I snap. "What you're talking about . . ." I shake my head.

"How did it happen?" Kernel asks. "I believe you, Beranabus — at least I think I do — but how? You always said the past was the one thing we could never change."

"It is. I mean, it was. Demons can't do it. Magicians certainly can't. But the *Kah-Gash* . . ."

Kernel draws his breath in sharply. "Are you sure?"

"It has to be," Beranabus insists. "The ultimate power . . . the ability to destroy an entire universe . . . Why not the potential to reverse time too?"

"But if you're right, that means . . ."

"Grubbs and Bec were the missing pieces. And there must have only been three. It couldn't have worked unless all the pieces were assembled. At least I don't think it could. . . ." He frowns.

"What the hell are you talking about?" I hiss. "What's a *Car Gash*?"

"Kah-Gash," Kernel corrects me. He's trembling, but not from the pain or cold. "It's a mythical weapon. You're meant to be able to destroy a universe with it, ours or the Demonata's. It was split into an unknown number of pieces millions or billions of years ago. Various demons and magicians have searched for it since then, without success. Thirty years ago we discovered one of the pieces. In me."

"You'd been implanted with something?"

"No. I *am* a piece of the Kah-Gash."

"I don't understand. How can you be part of a weapon? You're human."

"I'm magical," he disagrees. "The Kah-Gash is a weapon of magic, not physics. It can take the form of anything it chooses."

I think that through, putting it together with what they were saying a few minutes ago. "You believe Bec and I are part of this weapon too?"

"You have to be," Beranabus says. "The stars don't lie — we've gone back in time, to the night the tunnel was re-opened. You three did it. We saw it happening. No force in either universe could have accomplished that, except the Kah-Gash."

"How?" Kernel whispers. "And why? If this is the work of the Kah-Gash, where did it find the energy to alter the flow of time? And why bring us back to this specific moment? Why stop here, not a hundred years ago or a million? Why not shatter the laws of time entirely?"

Beranabus scratches the back of his neck. "What did you feel when it was happening?" he asks.

Kernel shrugs. "Great power flowing into me."

"From where?"

"All around."

"Grubbs? Can you be any more specific?"

"The ground," I mutter. "The power came from the rocks, from beneath."

"And did it flow into you or through you?"

"What's the difference?"

"You'd have exploded if you drew in that much energy and didn't let it out," Beranabus says. "You had to channel the magic. But where to? The demons? The sky? Where?"

"The cave," Kernel answers after several seconds of thoughtful silence. "The power came from the ground, then went through us, back down into the rock, to the cave . . . the tunnel."

"Yes," I agree, thinking back.

Beranabus smiles. "The Kah-Gash — you, Kernel, and Bec — acted as a kind of magnifying lens. You drew energy from the tunnel, then focused it back." He goes to stroke his beard, realizes he doesn't have one, and taps his chin instead. "I can't be sure — maybe I never will be — but this is how I think it worked.

"Opening a window between the Demonata's universe and ours is like making a hole in a dam — matter flows from their universe to ours, generating energy. Space, time, gravity, the forces that hold our universes together . . . they seep across every time a demon or one of us makes a rip.

"Windows are small, temporary. The energy generated is minimal. But in this case a tunnel was created, open twenty-four hours a day. A huge river of magic flowed through. You three tapped into that. No . . . you must have done more than tap into it. You . . ." He clicks his fingers. "You rode it! It was like a wave of energy. You caught the wave and rode it back to its source, converting and channeling it at the same time."

"Rode it back to its source?" Kernel echoes. "You mean back to the universe of the Demonata?"

"No," Beranabus says. "You followed the wave back in time, transforming it and eradicating it, back to when the tunnel was created." He looks at me. His eyes are bright with excitement. "This is the night of the full moon. The night Lord Loss returned to Carcery Vale. The Kah-Gash brought us back in time to the night when the tunnel was re-activated, *so that we could prevent it from ever being opened in the first place!*"

He seizes my hands and squeezes tight. "Don't you see? We've been given a second chance. Not just to heal the damage done by the demons, but to stop it from happening at all."

"But . . . no . . . it can't . . ." I mutter, head spinning.

"Grubbs," Beranabus says softly. "At this time, Dervish and your brother are still alive. We can help them, but only if we accept this and act fast. Now, are you going to stand there denying what your senses tell you, or are you going to help me save the world and all the people you love?"

And when he puts it like that . . .

# TIMELY INTERVENTION

✦ ✦ ✦

BERANABUS has entered the hole but has only advanced to the point where it widens into the shaft. He's squatting there, eyes closed, sensing the cave beneath, determining exactly who and what we have to fight.

I wish we'd traveled back another few days. We could have called on the Disciples for support. But Beranabus said we couldn't have come back any further. Because we were riding the wave of energy generated by the opening of the tunnel, we could only follow it back to its origin. He likened it to coming to the end of a train line — when you run out of track, that's it, end of ride.

There's been no sign of Bec. I've kept a close eye on the rocks and listened for her strange whispers, but she hasn't shown. I know Beranabus is concerned for her. He thinks she might have perished to help send us back, sacrificed herself for our sake. I don't see the big deal if she did — she was dead already! — but I don't say that to Beranabus. That girl seems to be the one person in the world he gives a damn about. I doubt he'd appreciate wisecracks at her expense.

Kernel is walking around, hands by his sides, trying to navigate like a bat. Only instead of emitting radar beams (or whatever bats emit), he sends out magical impulses, which bounce back, letting him know what's around him. At least that's the theory — but with all the trees he's crashed into during the last few minutes, I'm not sure it works.

"Ouch!" Kernel bumps into another low-hanging branch and steps back, rubbing his head.

"Why don't you give it a rest?" I snap. "You'll poke —"

I brake to a halt. I'd been about to say he'd poke an eye out if he wasn't careful, but I guess it's a bit late for warnings like that.

"I have to learn," Kernel mutters. "Beranabus needs me. There are demons to kill."

I walk over to him, take his left arm, and gently guide him clear of the trees. His courage fills me with awe and shame. Sure, I found the guts to pitch in when there was no other option, but this is bravery of a different kind. He's just lost his eyes, yet here he is, determined to keep on fighting. In his shoes I'd be moaning like a baby, full of self-pity, seizing the opportunity to take a backseat and keep out of trouble.

"I'll direct you," I promise. "I'll be your eyes in the cave. Focus on your magic. I'll tell you where to aim it when the time's right."

"Thanks," he says, smiling faintly. "But I might as well practice while we're waiting. It can't hurt and it keeps my mind off what's happened. Besides, I think I'm getting the hang of it now." Prizing himself free, he starts walking again, arms rigid, face composed, senses alert.

"Ouch!"

✚ Scrabbling sounds. Beranabus emerges, brushing dirt and small stones off his unprotected skin. He doesn't look too worried — happy even, in a guarded kind of way. "It's better than I dared hope," he says. "Lord Loss and Juni are there, some of his familiars — the three we encountered on the plane — and Dervish and Bill-E. But that's all, unless others are masking their presence, which is unlikely. I think we only have five enemies to deal with." He makes a clicking noise with his tongue. "Or seven."

"Meaning what?" I snap.

"We don't know where Dervish and Bill-E stand."

"Of course we do," I retort. "They're on our side."

"Probably. But we mustn't count on it. We don't know how far into their minds Juni wormed herself. If they've fallen under her spell, they might be acting on the demon master's behalf."

"Never," I growl.

Beranabus shrugs. "I won't argue. Just be aware of the threat. I'm not saying we go down there and blow their heads off. But we might have to knock them around a bit."

"I know Dervish and Bill-E," I say tightly. "They wouldn't betray us, no matter how strong the spell."

"Don't be naive," Beranabus barks, then calls Kernel in close. "Will you be all right down there or are you just going to get in our way?"

I think it's hugely insensitive of him to speak to his blind assistant like that, but Kernel only smiles. "I'll be fine. Grubbs will give me a helpful shove in the right direction. I can't do much, but I can make a nuisance of myself."

"As long as you're a nuisance for them, not us," Beranabus grunts, then lowers his voice. "Let's not get overly confident. There might be only five of them, but they're a deadly quintet. Lord Loss is more powerful than any of us. Juni's a match for Kernel even with eyes — she's certainly stronger than him now. And the familiars are dangerous too. Let's not forget we're an old man, his blind assistant, and a kid who could do anything under pressure."

"You sure know how to steady a guy's nerves before a fight," I note sarcastically.

"I'm not here to make uplifting speeches," Beranabus replies. "We have a good chance to win. The odds are far better than they were before. But we have to be sharp. We can't afford any mistakes. We've been handed a second chance — there won't be a third. We've seen what the consequences are if we lose. So let's stay focused and give it the very best we have. And remember, if we lose, we die, and everybody else in the world will too."

He starts to rise, then stops. "I almost forgot the most important point." He chuckles at himself. "I'm too old and senile to protect the world any longer. If we get through this, it'll be time to invest in a pair of slippers and find some quiet corner of the globe where I can . . ."

He coughs. "Sorry. Lost my train of thought. What was I saying?"

"The most important point," Kernel reminds him patiently.

"Aye. The key." He taps the ground to signify the importance of his next few words. "I explained earlier how the tunnel was opened. One of Lord Loss's human allies made a sacrifice in the cave and now has to join with the rock, to create the opening. Unless there's somebody down there I don't know about, that person — the key — must be the woman who calls herself Juni Swan."

"Couldn't it be Artery or one of the other familiars?" I ask.

"No. It has to be a human. Those are the rules."

"Rules can change," Kernel says. "According to Bec, you were wrong about the demons being sucked back to their own universe if the tunnel was closed again."

"Aye," Beranabus growls irritably, "but she didn't mention anything about this rule changing. Besides, we saw Lord Loss and his familiars during the fight. Juni's the only one who wasn't present."

"It could be Dervish or the boy," Kernel suggests.

I stiffen, but before I can respond, Beranabus says, "No. If they're under the woman's spell, they only succumbed recently. Lord Loss planned to open the tunnel during the night of the previous full moon. That means the sacrifice had been made some weeks before. Dervish and the boy were definitely in control of their senses then. So it has to be Juni. She's our primary target. If we kill her, we win."

"Can't Lord Loss use another human instead?" I ask.

"No. Only the one who made the sacrifice can serve as the key. He could try again later and get someone else to make another sacrifice. But if we beat him tonight, we'll take steps to ensure he never has that option.

"Juni's the one we go for. Her companions will do everything they can to protect her. We'll have to fight them, but we mustn't let them distract us. Juni is the target. The others don't matter.

"So, you know what we have to do? Are you ready for one more battle, the most important ever? Are you primed to go boldly into the breach and grind these demons into the dirt?" He grabs my right hand and Kernel's left. "Are you with me, boys, all the way to the glorious, victorious end?"

"That's more like it." I grin.

"Exactly what you want to hear before you step into the gladiatorial pit," Kernel agrees.

We enjoy the moment, smiling at one another. (Kernel smiles a little off to the side, at a nearby tree.) Then we face the entrance to the cave and take a decisive step forward.

"Hold it!" I gasp, ruining the mood, but struck by a sudden thought that I can't let pass.

"What's wrong?" Beranabus asks.

"Nothing. I mean . . . I don't know if you can . . . it's no big deal, but . . ." I nod at my naked flesh. "I don't want to face them like this. You couldn't conjure up some clothes, could you?"

Beranabus stares at me in disbelief — then laughs. "The things you worry about! But, in a way, you're right. One should always go into battle suitably clad." He waves a hand regally and the trees rustle overhead. I have the sensation of being wrapped up tight by rough blankets. Looking down, I see that I'm clad from neck to ankles in a suit of green, brown, red, and yellow leaves, as are Beranabus and Kernel.

"The best I can do in a pinch," Beranabus says. "The material won't hold for long, but it should see us through the fight."

"Perfect." I smile, shaking my arms to make sure I'm not bound too tightly. Then we face the hole, take a step forward onto the slope and then down.

✠ The shaft feels narrower than before. The rock's hot to the touch and it seems to throb with magical energy. I climb silently in the darkness, searching for toeholds and fingerholds, careful not to send any pebbles tumbling in case the noise alerts the demons.

I hate this. No excitement at the thought of the battle to come. Just sheer terror. If there was any way to avoid it, I'd be out of here in a flash. But there are no alternatives. It's fight to the death or surrender this world and everyone I care about to the Demonata. I'd like to think I'm a hero, but the truth is I'm just doing what I have to. There isn't a choice.

Can I kill Juni if the opportunity falls my way? I'm not certain. I despise her, maybe even more than Lord Loss. He's a demon, born to be evil, but she made a conscious decision to betray her people. At the same time, she's human. It wouldn't be like killing a demon. I don't know if I could do it. Hopefully, I won't have to. Beranabus is the man for that job, and I imagine he'll relish the task of terminating the treacherous Miss Swan. But if things don't work out that way . . . if I come face-to-face with her . . . if it falls to me to finish her off . . .

I drive the thought away. No point worrying about it. I'll just have to play this out and hope for the best. I've got to go in there focused on the fight, confident of victory, not filled with doubt.

I concentrate on the climb and our crablike descent, hand by hand, foot by foot, slowly, carefully, edging ever closer to the demons below.

✠ We reach the bottom and group together on the solid cave floor. I can see light ahead of us. Soft, blue, unnatural. Three distinct, separate sounds —

Someone chanting.

Occasional growls and snapping noises.

Whimpering and moaning.

Beranabus checks that we're ready, then advances. I keep a few steps behind, slightly to his right so I can see ahead of him, guiding Kernel by his leaf-clad arm. I stub my toes on rocks with almost every step I take, but that's a minor pain, easily ignored.

We enter the main cave and the scene unfolds before us. Juni and Lord Loss are in front of the crack close to the waterfall, the crack *I* made. Momentary guilt — have I inadvertently helped the demons? But it doesn't last. Logic tells me not to worry. They could have created a similar opening without much effort.

A few yards behind Juni and her master, Dervish and Bill-E are kneeling, arms bound by ropes, gags in mouths. Artery, Femur, and Spine are dancing around them, cackling, making sudden lunges, teeth snapping, claws extended — then pulling away before making contact. Bill-E's the one whimpering and moaning, trying to squirm away from the demons.

Dervish is kneeling upright, glaring hatefully at Lord Loss and Juni, beaten but defiant.

Instant relief — Dervish and Bill-E are innocent. They haven't been bewitched by Juni. They're victims, not adversaries. A weight lifts from my heart. Whether or not I can kill Juni, there's no way I could have harmed my uncle or brother, even if they'd been working in league with the demons.

"Good evening, all!" Beranabus booms, startling me almost as much as the others in the cave. Lord Loss, his familiars, and Juni whirl round. Dervish and Bill-E's heads twist as far as the ropes allow. "I trust we're not late," Beranabus says, striding forward, saluting Dervish. "Got delayed en route. You'd never believe our story if we told you."

The rabbit-shaped Femur snarls and crouches, meaning to use its powerful hind legs to leap across the cave at Beranabus and splatter him with acid.

"Wait," Lord Loss stops the familiar. He taps Juni's left arm with one of his eight hands and nods at the crack. She shoots us a hateful glance, then faces the rock and resumes her chant. "This is an unexpected pleasure," Lord Loss says icily, drifting past Dervish and Bill-E and toward us.

"When we heard about the party, we had to drop in," Beranabus quips, very different from his normal, serious self. "I hope we're not unwelcome?"

"Certainly not," Lord Loss smiles. "I am delighted to see you. Especially young Grubitsch. I thought, when he slipped through our clutches on the airplane, that it might be a long time before our paths crossed again. Yet here he is, fresh and wide-eyed, ready to die. And you know you'll die, don't you, Grubitsch? You realize time has run out, that you, your uncle, and your brother are doomed?"

"Shut up, you ba —"

I stop abruptly. He called Bill-E my brother. Of course Lord Loss knew about that — Bill-E was infected with the family curse — but Bill-E didn't. We never told him. I try looking past the demon master, to catch my half brother's gaze, but Lord Loss is blocking the view.

"Yes, Grubitsch," the monster purrs. "I told him. We spent quite an amount of time tonight discussing how you kept the truth from him and ran away when the going got tough, leaving him behind for me as an offering."

"That's not true!" I shout. "Don't believe him, Bill-E. I —"

"That's not important now," Beranabus interrupts. "I want to know who's the mastermind behind this? What foul hell spawn are you working for? Who organized the demons and gave them orders to come running when the tunnel opens?"

Lord Loss frowns. "You know about our plan?"

"Obviously. Now tell me who's behind it."

The demon master chuckles. "No, Beranabus. You have been very clever. But if you do not know the full magnitude of the force you've chosen to pit yourself against, I will not enlighten you. It's not my job to explain. Do your own detective work. I am sure you and your capable assistants can . . ."

He pauses, catching sight of the eyeless Kernel Fleck. "But what is this? What happened to poor Cornelius?"

"Never mind," Beranabus snaps. "I want to know about —"

"I recognize those wounds," Lord Loss continues, raising his voice. "Those are the marks of my familiar, Spine. Such trademark injuries are unmistakable. I can even see some of his maggoty offspring embedded in the bloodied pits. It must have been a recent attack. But Spine has been with me the whole time." He looks back at his familiar. The scorpion with the semi-human face stares at him blankly.

"And your hair," Lord Loss says, facing us again. "You're as hairless as myself. You've been in a fight of great viciousness. Spine seems to have been in it too. But how . . . ?"

"Tell us about the demon who put you up to this and I'll tell you about our fight." Beranabus grins.

"If I thought you were genuine, I'd happily make that deal," Lord Loss replies. "I sense great magic and mystery in this. If I did not know better, I would say . . ." He trails off into silence, then sneers. "But I know you, Beranabus. You are a rogue. You would renege on your promise and tell me nothing. So I'll hold my tongue and torture the truth out of the boys once I've defeated you."

"Nay," Beranabus snorts. "Secrecy and surprise were the only advantages you had. Now that we've thwarted you, you must face us openly, on our world, where your powers are diminished. You can't beat us. If you abandon the spells and leave, I'll let you walk away and settle for sealing this place off. But if you force us to fight, we'll kill you all. Even those of you who have died before."

"Ah," Lord Loss chuckles. "You've seen through Miss Swan's disguise."

"I knew her for a cuckoo the moment I laid eyes on her," Beranabus says as Juni continues to chant, not glancing around even though she's the subject of their conversation.

"It took me awhile to pierce the illusion, but I knew of her true face long before she moved against Grubbs."

"What are you talking about?" I mutter.

"Watch," Beranabus says, and murmurs the words of a quick spell, waving a hand at Juni. Lord Loss makes no move to defend her. He's loving this. As I stare at Juni, her flesh ripples. She stops chanting and cries out, but with surprise, not pain. Her hands dart to her face and she turns sharply, flashing a furious glare at Beranabus. Dervish gives a muffled cry of shock and jerks away from her.

Her face has changed completely. Much plainer. Bad acne scars. Dirty short blond hair. Blue eyes. A sullen expression. Quite fat. Pale skin, but not as white as her albino flesh. She appears younger than before, maybe mid to late twenties.

"What's happening?" Kernel asks.

Before I can tell him, Juni shrieks in a voice entirely unlike her own, "Give me back my face, you swine!"

Kernel's forehead creases. "*Nadia?*" He gasps.

"You have a good ear," Lord Loss purrs. "Shame about the eyes."

"Nadia Moore," Beranabus snorts. "Another distant relative of yours, Grubbs, and once one of my closest assistants. I thought she died in Lord Loss's kingdom many years ago, but it seems she merely switched allegiances and created a new look for herself."

"Cornelius knew," Lord Loss says with relish. "Not about her rebirth as Juni Swan, but about her survival, the trick she pulled to escape your tyrannical rule. He kept it a secret from you, Beranabus. Perhaps he has other secrets. Are you certain you can trust him?"

Beranabus sniffs away the jibe. "I prefer you this way, Nadia," he says. "Reality's more attractive than facade. You should have kept your original face."

"I'm not Nadia Moore," Juni snarls. "She died, just the way you saw it. I put everything about her behind me — her name, features, loyalties. I'm Juni Swan now and always will be, even if you've disabled my glamour."

"I felt guilty when you were killed," Beranabus says softly. "About as guilty as I've ever felt in my long, wretched life. But I won't feel anything when you die a second time, when I kill you myself." His expression hardens and he addresses Lord Loss. "My offer stands. Walk away now and we won't interfere — I'll even let Nadia leave too. If you stay, you die."

"A generous offer," Lord Loss says. "If you had the backing of your Disciples, perhaps I'd be inclined to accept and slaughter you another time — I prefer to fight when the odds are in my favor. But you come only with a blind boy and a cur who has already proved his cowardice. And though you yourself are a fearsome opponent, you're only one man. And no man, no matter how powerful, has ever gotten the better of a demon master. So, in answer to your offer . . ."

Lord Loss smirks vilely, then screeches unintelligibly at his familiars. With ear-piercing howls of delight, the demons attack.

# THE HIGH . . .

✤     ✤     ✤

ARTERY and Lord Loss hurl themselves at Beranabus. The scorpion-shaped Spine targets Kernel, eager to finish the job that it doesn't remember starting. Femur sets its sights on me.

It's almost comical watching the rabbit bound toward me. It's like a sick cartoon, Bugs Bunny gone batty, leaping on people to plant a great smacker of a kiss on them. Except this creature's acidic smooch will melt a person's face and leave him a smoldering, sizzling mess — not the sort of fare you'd usually find in a Looney Tunes flick.

Femur spits acid in midair. It spurts toward me, a sheet of liquid death. Directed by the magic inside me, I wave my left hand at the deadly juice. It divides and hisses past my head, hitting a couple of stalagmites behind me, quickly eating into them and eroding the work of thousands of years.

The rabbit's leap brings it within reach. I grab its neck and twist sharply. The neck breaks and I toss the creature away. It gurgles, then heals itself and gets up. I smile, grown bold by the combination of magic and ease with which I shrugged off the demon's attack. I beckon to it. "Try again, lettuce muncher!"

As Femur tenses its rear legs and works its lips over its gums, Kernel stumbles past me. Spine is on his head, jabbing its stinger at his eye sockets. He's batting it away. "Let me know if you need help!" I shout. Then Femur leaps and spits acid again, and I have to focus on that.

As I fend off the rabbit I spot Beranabus. Lord Loss has the magician within his grasp, all eight arms wrapped around him, a spider devouring a fly. Artery is on Beranabus's back, chewing at his shoulders. One of his hands is under the magician's skin. I see knuckles moving within the flesh.

Maybe it's a trick of the light, but Beranabus's skin appears to be a different color. There's a purple tinge to it, and his eyes seem to have grown and turned a dark grey shade. And the blood streaming from the hole in his shoulder that Artery's chewing at . . . is it *yellow?*

As I'm studying Beranabus uncertainly, Femur bounces up once more, spraying its corrosive poison. Snapping back to attention, I freeze the acid, then punch through the solid panel of ice and grab the rabbit's ears. "Enough of this crap," I grunt, and drive my left fist down the demon's throat.

Femur's eyes bulge alarmingly. It chokes and tries to gnaw through my arm. Cuts the flesh up pretty bad. Pain flares, but I numb myself to it and focus on my hand deep in the rabbit's guts. I fill the fist with magic, then let it explode, incinerating the demon from the inside out. Femur gasps, mouth slackening, blinking furiously. Its legs shake. Acid dribbles over my forearm, but I turn it to mist before it harms me.

The rabbit's ears rip loose and I throw them away. They flop around on the floor of the cave for a few seconds, then fall still as life leaves Femur's body. Its flesh turns a dark red color, then crumbles away like ash. I pull my arm free and study the mess, lips curled with disgust. I start toward the waterfall to wash myself clean and sluice out my wounds. Then I have a better idea and direct magic at my arm. Seconds later — spotless, unmarked flesh. Coolio!

My first thought is to go to Beranabus's aid or help Kernel with Spine. But then the magician's warning kicks in. Juni Swan is public enemy number one. She has to be stopped. I'm not sure I can do it — the doubts swim back inside my head — but I have to try.

Skirting Beranabus and Lord Loss, I hurry to where the transformed Juni is chanting into the crack, arms spread wide, words coming fast and furious. For a second I think I glimpse a face in the rock, just within the opening of the crack. But then it's gone and I'm not sure whether it was Bec, the first of the demon hordes, or a trick of the light.

I don't want to touch Juni — the thought of physical contact with her repulses me. So I bring my hands together and summon a bolt of magic to fire instead. Nothing happens. I can feel the magic, but it's like there's a barrier between us, blocking the lines of communication. Then I realize what the problem is — the werewolf. There's a full moon. Beranabus told me I'd have no trouble suppressing the wolf now, but it would always be there, scratching away beneath the surface, whining, trying to break free.

"No time for games, wolfie," I mutter, and mentally drive the beast deep down within me, to howl in silent, imprisoned protest for at least another month. The magic burns brightly inside me as soon as the way's been cleared. Once again I tell it what I want, and this time I feel energy gather in my hands. Pointing them at Juni, I unleash the power. A huge ball of magic shoots straight at her — then hits an invisible barrier and crackles away into nothing.

Juni glances around, sneers at me, keeps on chanting.

"'Ubbs!" Dervish grunts as I prepare a second blast. He's straining to get to his feet. Beside him, Bill-E's staring at me as if he doesn't know who I am. "'Ubbs!" Dervish shouts again, mouth constricted by his gag.

I wave a hand at my uncle and brother. Their gags and the ropes binding them burn away. As soon as he's free, Dervish thrusts himself up and throws his arms around me. "I thought you were dead!" he cries, burying his head in my chest.

"Not me," I grin, hugging back hard, momentarily forgetting the fight and all that's at stake. It's so great to see him again, to have him hold me, to be home and with the closest thing to a father I have left. If the world ended here and now, for me it would be a good end.

"Grubbs?" Bill-E says hesitantly, studying me warily. "Is it really you?"

"Sure is . . . little brother." I smile at him awkwardly.

"You should have told me," he growls, pointing a finger. "All this time . . . if I'd known . . . all my life I thought I was alone. You should have told me!"

"I know," I sigh. "I was a fool. Forgive me?"

"No way, baldy," he smirks. The smile quickly fades when he spots the woman next to the crack. *"Her!"* he growls, finger swiveling. "Is that Juni?"

"Yes," Dervish snarls. "The face might be different, but the evil stench is the same. She told us you attacked her, Grubbs. That after killing Ma and Pa Spleen, you . . ." He pauses. "You didn't kill them, did you?"

"Of course not," I huff indignantly, not admitting that I'd thought the same thing myself.

"I told you," Bill-E says proudly. "I knew Grubbs wasn't a murderer."

"I didn't think so either," Dervish mutters. "But she was so convincing. Sobbed hard when she came back. Said she saw you murder them, that you tried to kill Billy, but she lured you away. She was a pillar of strength. Guided us through the burials. Comforted Billy. Helped deal with the police inquiries. I loved her more than ever.

"Then she said we could find you, that she could use the magic of this cave to locate you. Fool that I was, I believed her. Billy had moved in with us. Juni said we should bring him along, that it might help with the spell. I didn't see how, but she was stronger than me. She knew more about magic. I trusted her.

"When we got here, the demons jumped us. Juni clubbed me over the back of my head and they trussed us up. Lord Loss told us he was going to open the tunnel. A sacrifice had been made, and the killer would join with the rock and keep the tunnel open. He said he'd let the Demonata cross, then murder me slowly. Said he had something extra special in mind for Billy. He —"

"Dervish," I interrupt softly. "If she finishes that spell, we're in for seventy-seven different types of hell. We need to kill her. *Now.*"

Dervish nods grimly. "OK. You work on bringing down the barrier. I'll handle the rest."

"You're sure?" I ask, grateful that he's offering to take the horrible task out of my hands but wanting to provide him with an alternative if he feels he can't slaughter the woman he once loved.

"I'd fight anybody who tried to kill her before I had a shot," Dervish says, and the burning hatred in his expression scares me.

One quick glance behind me. Kernel's pinned Spine to a stalagmite and wrapped the demon's stinger around the needle of calcium. He's pummeling its face with his right fist, holding the tip of the stinger in place with his left hand.

Beranabus — his flesh an even darker shade of purple than before — is locked in combat with Lord Loss, the demon master howling like a dog, the snakes in his chest cavity lashing the magician with their forked tongues. Artery has worked both hands under Beranabus's skin and is trying to get his head in too, to chew his way through the bones and into the meaty innards. It's not looking good for the old magician, but I know he would rather we killed Juni and let him perish than go to his rescue and leave her free to open the tunnel.

I let magical energy charge within my fists again — *blast!* Charge — *blast!* Charge — *blast!* Dervish is standing a few feet ahead of me, out of the way of the explosions, fingers twitching, eyes locked on Juni, eager to squeeze his hands around her throat. Bill-E is watching my back, keeping track of the demons, making sure none springs on me unawares.

The barrier starts to give. Each ball of magic crackles louder and lasts longer when it smacks against the energy field. A few more and she'll be at our mercy.

"Master!" Juni screams. "Help me! I need more time!"

"Spine!" Lord Loss roars. "Femur!" I sense him looking for his familiars. Then he curses. "Attack them, Artery. Leave Beranabus to me."

Ripping sounds. Bill-E yells a warning. "Grubbs! Look out! He's —"

Artery lands on my back and I stagger. Before I can turn to deal with the hell child, Dervish grabs his legs, swings him around, and batters his head off a low-hanging stalactite. The skull splits down the middle and brains ooze out. Lice fall from the fiendish baby's crown and scuttle around on the ground. Dervish twirls the demon overhead a couple of times, then throws him far across the cave, where he smashes hard into a wall and collapses. Artery will recover, but it'll take him a minute or two. That should be more than enough time.

"Master!" Juni screams again, spitting the cry out between the words of the spell that she's chanting. Her real face looks far less commanding than the one she wore when she was pretending to be our friend. It carries the scars of fear and low character. "One more minute. That's all I need."

Lord Loss howls louder than any wolf, then reluctantly releases Beranabus and whacks him aside. I hear a whoosh as he propels himself toward me. "Grubbs!" Dervish yells.

"Just a second," I mumble, taking aim, letting off one last blast of energy. It sounds like a gunshot when it hits the barrier — then crashes through and connects with Juni, knocking her to the floor.

I open my mouth to cheer, but Lord Loss is on me before I can, cursing foully, eight arms around my mouth and throat, squeezing, tearing, intent on pulling me to pieces and choking me all at once.

Gasping for air, I grab two of his arms, focus my magic, and tug with all my strength. The arms rip free of their sockets. Lord Loss wails and tries to reattach them, but I send fire shooting up the limbs and they burn away to nothing before he can restore them.

Dervish steps in to help. "No!" I yell, feet dangling a few inches above the ground as a furious Lord Loss clutches me to his chest, where the snakes fight with one another to bite out my eyes. "Kill Juni! I can deal with —"

The demon master gets a few mangled, lumpy, bloody fingers into my mouth. They lengthen and extend back into my throat. Out of the corner of my eye, I see Dervish wavering. His natural instinct is to help me. But then he sees Juni back on her feet, muttering the spell again. With a wild curse he goes after her.

I bite off the fingers and spit them out. Lord Loss screams obligingly. One of the snakes digs its fangs into my bald skull and rips out a chunk of flesh. I snatch the snake from its heartless home and chew its head off. I'm starting to enjoy this biting business.

Lord Loss's six remaining arms tighten around my body. I feel the bones of my rib cage creak and groan. I know that if the demon maintains this pressure, the bones will snap and pierce my lungs and heart, and that will be the end of me. But it doesn't matter. I'm buying time for Dervish. Stopping Juni is my only reason for being here, for living. If I have to die to thwart her evil plans, that's just bad luck. I'll give my life gladly.

But before I can die nobly, Beranabus stumbles back into action. Picking up a stone, he invests it with magic and hurls it at Lord Loss's head. The stone pierces the demon master's flesh and bone and ends up sticking half in and half out of the monster's skull, just above his left ear.

Lord Loss shrieks with pain and rage, then twirls and throws me at Beranabus. I collide with the magician and we sprawl across the ground. Lord Loss starts after us, then remembers Juni. Hesitating, he looks over his shoulder. Juni's wrestling with Dervish, shouting the spell even as they battle. Dervish is striking her hard, weeping, hands clenched together to form one mighty club. Juni's pockmarked, pasty face has been smashed to a pulp. Her hair and skin are flecked with blood, and her eyes are almost invisible behind her mashed flesh.

As Lord Loss turns to help, she stops chanting and smiles at Dervish. Her flesh ripples, changes color, and she looks like the old Juni Swan again, only battered and bleeding. "Dervish, my love," she wheezes. "Please stop. You're hurting poor Juni."

"You betrayed us!" Dervish roars, tears coming harder than ever.

"I made a mistake," Juni murmurs. "I love you, Dervish. Please don't hurt me. I can make this right if you give me the chance."

Dervish stares at her, hands dropping, fury leaving his body, shoulders sagging. He takes a step forward. I think he means to hug her. That scares me but not as much as what I suddenly spot happening overhead — the rock around the crack has started to pulse! Light is shining from deep within. And it's beginning to split wider apart.

"Dervish!" I yell. "She finished the spell. The demons are coming. You have to kill her!"

Dervish stops moving but doesn't bring his hands together. Beranabus throws himself forward desperately. Lord Loss grabs him and laughs.

Skittering footsteps behind me. I half turn and spot Artery leaping, three sets of sharp teeth gnashing savagely. I raise my arms — too late. The demon strikes me in the chest with his tiny feet. I fly across the cave and smash into the rock at the back of the waterfall. Come up spluttering and cold, my leaf suit soaked through and disintegrating, the water cutting out the sounds and sights of the cave.

I drag myself clear of the waterfall as Artery bounds toward me. He leaps to kick me again, but this time I grab him by his childish torso and hold him at arm's length, trying to find the strength to kill him but too exhausted and dispirited. I glance around wearily, looking for help or inspiration.

Kernel is still out of the main action, unable to kill Spine, struggling to keep the demon pinned to the stalagmite. Lord Loss is bearing down mercilessly on Beranabus, squeezing tightly, snakes more active than ever. The demon master is laughing triumphantly, confident of victory. The opening in the rock is pulsing faster and faster, the colors and shades of light changing with every pulse, the mouth of the crack stretching, widening, extending. A magic-laced wind whistles up out of nowhere. I feel it blowing past me, toward the hole. Soft at first, but growing steadily, sucking up dust and bits of grit, sending them shooting down the crack. Bill-E's scrabbling away from the hole, moaning, sensing disaster.

And just beneath the crack — what will soon be the entry point for hundreds of demons — Juni Swan is kissing Dervish, her luminous white hair billowing out in a fan shape, gusting away from her skull in the ever-increasing breeze.

"My love," Juni gurgles, pulling back from him slightly, pink eyes twinkling maliciously. She strokes his cheeks, smiles seductively, kisses him again. Dervish is motionless, mesmerized, under her spell. Moving her head to his shoulder, she murmurs into his throat, "You could never harm your Juni. You love me, as I love you. What savagery, hitting me like that. But I forgive you. I love you too much to bear a grudge."

Her fake flesh has already healed and is as smooth and white as ever, though a few streaks of blood remain. She looks beautiful. It's strange, but unconcealed evil suits her. She's more stunning now than she ever was when she was pretending to be good.

I try shouting a warning, but I don't have the strength. Holding Artery at bay is all I can manage.

"I'll take you to the universe of the Demonata when this is over," Juni promises Dervish. "You'll have to be killed eventually, but there's no rush. I'll show you such wonders and treat you so sweetly, you won't care about dying. In fact you'll die gladly, to please me. Won't you, my love?"

Dervish stares at her blankly. Then Bill-E screams. "Dervish! I'm afraid!"

Juni laughs. "Don't worry, silly Billy, I haven't forgotten about you. How could I? You're the most important —"

Dervish grabs Juni by the waist and picks her up as if she's weightless. *"No!"* she screams, lashing out at him but unable to connect because of the angle he's holding her at. Dervish lunges away from the pulsing rock, struggling against the wind. Juni's hands stretch upward, searching for magic. Her lips start on a new spell. Lord Loss shouts with alarm and springs away from Beranabus.

But Dervish is too quick for both of them. He looks around. Takes a couple of steps to his right, holding Juni high above his head. Then slams her down with all his strength on top of a small stalagmite.

The tip pierces Juni's flesh and slices in through the skin of her back — then bursts through her chest a moment later. Dervish cries out and falls away, staring with wonder and disbelief at Juni as blood spurts and her legs and arms thrash, as if he doesn't know how she got there.

"My swan!" Lord Loss howls, flying to her side.

"Master . . ." Juni groans, her mouth full of blood. "Help . . . me."

Lord Loss reaches out to her, then stops and studies the wound. He shakes his head softly, sorrowfully. "I cannot," he says.

Juni stares at him incredulously. Then her expression clears. "I understand. Thank you, master. For . . . everything you showed me . . . all that you did for me . . . I offer my everlasting gratitude . . . and love."

Lord Loss stretches out a single arm and touches Juni's cheek with his clammy fingers. He's smiling sadly, but it's not his usual mocking smile — this one is almost human. "I will miss you," he mutters.

"And I . . ." Juni shudders and her eyes go wide. "Death!" she wheezes. "It's here. I sense it. I . . . no! Don't let it take me, master! I want to be free. Don't . . ."

She stops. Her mouth and eyes freeze. Lord Loss bends, kisses her forehead, then floats back a few paces. "Goodbye, sweet swan," he murmurs, and that's when I know for sure she's dead, though it's not until I hear Beranabus chuckling softly that I realize what that means.

The key has been eliminated . . . The tunnel can't be opened . . . *We've won!*

# . . . AND THE LOW

✛　　✛　　✛

THE sweetness of a hard-won victory lasts all of two seconds. Maybe three. Then it hits me — the rocks within and around the crack are still pulsing. The lights are flashing more vibrantly than at a disco. The wind is growing stronger.

"Beranabus!" I yell. "Why isn't it stopping?"

"It is," he mutters, staring at the crack doubtfully. "It must be. We killed her. But sometimes it can take a minute for a body to properly die, for all the senses to expire. When the last spark of life flickers out in her, this will end."

"But if the demons cross before that . . ."

Beranabus shrugs, then winces and reaches back to try to heal the wounded flesh between his shoulder blades. His skin and eyes are normal now. He looks like a tired old man, not a mighty magician. "A few might squeeze through, but not many. We'll just have to —"

"Imbeciles," Lord Loss snorts. He glares at Beranabus, then Dervish, who's lying close by Juni. Her face has lost its glamour, changed back to its real appearance, scarred and bloody from the beating she took. Dervish is staring at her with a mix of horror and loss. "You think you have defeated us? You believe we fall that easily? You are arrogant and ignorant, Beranabus, the result of too many soft victories over lesser demons. Killing Juni won't save your pitiful excuse of a world — or your lives. It only makes me more determined to see you and the grotesque Gradys suffer slowly and agonizingly."

"We were wrong!" I roar. "The key wasn't Juni. It's one of the demons." I spin, trying to figure out whether it's Artery or Spine.

"It can't be," Beranabus pants, struggling to his feet. "It doesn't work that way, and we saw them both in the future."

"Then I was right," Lord Loss hisses. "You traveled back in time!" He stares at Beranabus, awestruck. "How did you do it? I thought *that*, of all things, was impossible. How —"

"Beranabus," I interrupt. "We have to kill them now, before the Demonata —"

"But it's not them," he insists. "We *saw* them."

"Then somebody else!" I holler. "Another human assistant, invisible, hidden by magic. We have to find him . . . her . . . whatever!"

Beranabus nods and stumbles away, feverishly scouring the cave with magic and his eyes. I start off in the opposite direction.

"Grubbs," Bill-E moans, crawling toward me, wind snapping at him, clothes and hair rippling, the crack threatening to suck him in.

"Not now. Dervish." My uncle doesn't respond. "Dervish!" I yell. He blinks and looks up. "The key's still alive. It wasn't

Juni. We have to find the person who made the sacrifice. If we don't, the tunnel will —"

"Grubbs," Bill-E moans again.

"Stop bugging me!" I scream, then stoop to look him in the eyes. "I'm sorry, but there isn't time. If we don't find the person who made the sacrifice, they'll merge with the rock and the demons will flood through and kill us all."

I stand. Bill-E clutches the sodden, straggly left leg of my makeshift trousers. I curse and kick his hand away. I'm turning to continue searching when he whispers something, too soft for me to decipher. I almost don't pause, but there's an urgency in the whisper that demands attention.

"What did you say?" I shout without looking down, eyes piercing the shadows of the cave. It's difficult to see. The lights inside the crack are throbbing more brightly, changing color swiftly. Bill-E repeats himself but again too softly for the words to carry. "Speak up, damn it. I don't have time for —"

"I think the key might be *me*," Bill-E croaks.

And for the second time within the space of an hour the world appears to stop.

✠ Staring at Bill-E. Certain I heard him wrong. Praying that if I heard him right, I misunderstood. "What?" I wheeze.

"I think . . . it wasn't intentional . . . I'm not sure . . . but . . ."

*He wasn't one of the dead,* a voice inside my head murmurs. *In the future, when you looked into the hole, you didn't see Bill-E. Dervish was there, Reni, most of the other people you cared about. But not your brother.*

"Oh, dear," Lord Loss snickers, floating out of reach,

expression twisting with malicious joy. "The penny drops at long, painful last."

"No." I gasp, the syllable whipped from my lips by the wind. "It can't be."

"Grubbs?" Dervish asks, seeing something fearful in my face.

"Grubbs!" Beranabus roars. He's a long way off. Doesn't know what's going on. "Make yourself busy, boy. We have to find the killer. There isn't much time left."

"But you've already found him, haven't you, Grubitsch?" Lord Loss teases.

"You're lying," I snarl.

Lord Loss shakes his head. "I never lie."

Bill-E falls flat on his stomach and slides toward the crack. Dervish grabs him and holds tight. I crouch beside them, ignoring Lord Loss's laughter and the bite of the demonic wind. I can hear the cries and chitterings of other demons, coming from a universe that isn't our own. I tune them out and focus on Bill-E. He's utterly terrified. I smile at him, and even though the smile's weak, he finds comfort in it, and in spite of his terror, he speaks.

"It was Loch," he mutters. "I hated the way he teased me, always making me feel small and worthless. He was a bully. You should have stood up to him, Grubbs. You're my big brother."

"I didn't want to fight your battles for you." I sense what he's going to tell me and I feel like crying, but tears won't come. I can't let them.

"Always teasing," Bill-E says sourly. "Making fun of me. Any excuse to take a dig. That day when we discovered the cave . . . you were sick . . . me and Loch went climbing in search of Lord Sheftree's treasure . . ."

It seems a lifetime ago. Did we really engage in such playful, innocent games? Was there truly a time when buried treasure seemed important, when a school bully was our only concern? Or did we dream it all?

"I saw a chance to get my own back," Bill-E continues, voice breaking. "We were near the top of the waterfall. He slipped and grabbed hold of a rock. He was clinging on by his fingertips. I stuck my hand out. He snatched for it. But then I . . . I . . . *I whipped my hand away!*"

Bill-E and I lock expressions. We both understand what he means. Dervish doesn't. He never saw Loch doing that very same thing to Bill-E at school, making him look like a fool in front of everybody. He's staring at us as if we're mad.

"I whipped it away," Bill-E says numbly. "Put my thumb on my nose. Said, 'Touché, sucker!' Stuck my tongue out. I didn't mean for him to fall. I just wanted to have a laugh. But he lost his grip. Fell before I could help him. Hit his head on the ground. His skull cracked open. He . . ."

Bill-E stops. His face is white. He's trembling. The wind pulls strongly at him — more strongly than at me, Dervish, or anybody else in the cave.

"No," I say calmly. "You didn't kill him. It wasn't a sacrifice. You aren't the key." But I know it's not true. Even as I deny it, I *know.*

"Grubbs," Dervish wheezes. "What are you saying? What does it mean? Are you mad? You think Bill-E caused this?"

"No," I lie. "Of course not." But putting the pieces together inside my head. The death — not an accident. Loch's blood vanishing into the floor of the cave. I'd forgotten about that, but I remember now, the bare floor, wondering where all the blood had gone. Now I know — sucked up by magic. Taken as sacrificial blood, even though it wasn't intended to be.

Bill-E guilty. By the strictest letter of the law he killed Loch Gossel, and the magic in this cave is holding him accountable. I should have suspected sooner. Beranabus kept a tight watch on the cave when he arrived. He couldn't understand how Juni slipped past him and made a sacrifice. Never suspected Bill-E. Took me at my word when I told him we were alone, that Loch died accidentally.

The demons had it easy. No need to slaughter one of their mages or even enter the cave and risk alerting Beranabus. A sweet deal. The sacrifice had already been made. All Lord Loss and Juni had to do was turn up a few weeks later, chant the correct spells, and make sure the *killer* was present.

Except they didn't know who that was. They thought it was me, that the beast or my magic made me murder. That's why Juni sent me to the cave the night I turned, why she took my blood and smeared the edges of the crack with it. When that failed to produce a reaction, they realized that Bill-E must be the guilty one. So Juni hurried over to his house, to haul him in. Nothing personal. It wasn't for revenge. Lord Loss wanted Bill-E solely for business. And he never meant to kill him. He had other plans for the younger Grady brother.

The wind increases. Dervish has to dig his heels in hard to

hold Bill-E back. He looks at me, panicking. "Grubbs! What can we do?"

That tells me he knows too and understands what must be done. He just doesn't want to admit it, because that would place the burden on him. He doesn't want the responsibility. Well, too bad — I don't want it either.

"Bill-E's the key," I tell him.

"No," Dervish protests, but weakly, unconvincingly.

"Grubbs!" Beranabus yells. "I hear them coming. What the hell are —"

"Bill-E's the key!" I scream, and Beranabus gapes at me. "He made the sacrifice. He didn't mean to. It was an accident. But —"

"You don't know what you're saying," Dervish hisses.

I look at him miserably. "Yes, I do."

"What's wrong?" Bill-E mutters, glancing from one of us to the other. "This is good, isn't it? Now that we know, we can cast a spell to stop it, can't we? Or . . . should I have kept my big mouth . . . shut?"

"No," I smile. "You did the right thing. Everything will be OK now. We can stop the demons. You're a hero. You've shown us the way to win."

Bill-E beams proudly. Dervish is staring at me awfully, trembling, gripping his chubby nephew tight. I turn hopelessly to Beranabus, maintaining the smile until I'm facing away from Bill-E, so he can't see the anguish in my eyes. "Is there another way?" I cry.

"No," Beranabus says, no pity in his voice, just determination. He starts across the cave, fingers flexing. But he's taken no more than three or four steps when Lord Loss drops into his path and fires a bolt of magic at him, forcing him back.

"No, no, no, Beranabus," the demon master coos. "I won't allow you to spoil such a fascinating scene. This is tremendous sport. Uncle and brother speared on the horns of a most grueling dilemma. What excruciating entertainment!"

Beranabus tries to respond with a magic bolt of his own, but Lord Loss hits him first. The magician collapses, defenses crumbling, all washed up.

The wind is a storm now. Bill-E's feet are rising into the air. Dervish won't be able to hold him much longer. Another minute, maybe less, then Bill-E will be torn into the crack, his flesh will join with the rock, and he'll become a living tunnel between this universe and the Demonata's.

"Dervish!" I scream.

"I can't."

"But the demons . . ."

"I know. But I can't." He pulls Bill-E to his chest and wraps both arms around him, fighting the storm, tears coursing down his cheeks.

"Grubbs," Bill-E grunts, jerking his head clear. "What's happening? What do we have to do?"

"Dervish," I say steadily, ignoring the question. "If you don't, we'll all die. Everybody else too. Including Bill-E. We can't save him."

"You do it then," Dervish challenges me.

"No. He's my brother."

"Do *what?*" Bill-E howls as Dervish and I glare at one another.

Then the fingers of Dervish's right hand creep up Bill-E's

back. They stop at his neck and spread, gripping the flesh tight. He hasn't broken eye contact with me. I'm crying, unable to hold back the tears any longer. Bill-E doesn't know what's happening. He looks at me, forehead creased, trying to make sense of this. I hope he doesn't. Better if he never knows, if Dervish does it quickly and it comes as a short, sharp surprise.

His right hand in place, Dervish moves his left hand up. I don't know if he means to choke Bill-E or snap his neck. And I never find out. Because the fingers halt halfway up Bill-E's spine.

"I can't," Dervish says quietly, and this time the words are the confession of a broken man.

"I knew it," Lord Loss laughs. "Humans are so predictable. Even though all else must fall, you cannot bring yourself to harm your beloved nephew. You'll damn yourself, him, the whole world, all because of misplaced love." He sighs happily. "Moments such as these make the long, monotonous millennia worthwhile."

Dervish moans and clutches Bill-E close, planning to hug him as long as he can, to maybe get sucked into the crack with him, so the pair can perish together. Except Bill-E won't die. He'll become something terrible and twisted, inhuman and beastlike.

I think of Bill-E suffering, captive within the rock, alive down here indefinitely, racked with guilt, a plaything for the Demonata when all the other humans have been slaughtered. They'll torment him. Guilt will eat him whole. Madness will be his only escape, but the demon masters will use magic to restore his senses, to torture him afresh. An eternity of misery, madness, and sorrow.

I can't let that happen.

Entering this cave, I realized I couldn't kill Dervish or Bill-E if they were in league with Lord Loss, not even to save the world. I still can't. But to save Bill-E from a fate genuinely worse than death . . . for my brother's sake, as opposed to the sake of billions of others who mean nothing to me . . .

"Bill-E." I lean forward, smiling. "Want to help me kick the crap out of these demon creeps?"

Bill-E returns the smile. "Now you're talking! What do we have to do?"

"Grubbs," Dervish groans.

"Shut up," I snap, then smile at Bill-E again. "Take my hands, little brother. Close your eyes. Focus on . . ." I gulp. "Your mom. Think of your mother."

"How can that help?" he asks doubtfully.

"It'll clear your head of bad thoughts and fear," I improvise. "I need your help to stop this. But I can only do it if you're calm. It won't be easy, but you have to try. Think of your mom and every good time you ever shared. That will generate a positive energy that I can channel. I can use that power to stop the demons."

"Brilliant!" Bill-E gasps, face lighting up. He sticks his hands out, shuts his eyes, and concentrates, lids twitching, eyeballs rolling behind them as he searches his memories for cherished moments. He trusts me completely.

Lord Loss has drifted closer. He could stop this, kill or delay me, but he's entranced. He's forgotten his mission of all conquering mayhem. Living only for the bittersweet pain of the moment. Dervish has lowered his face to Bill-E's shoulder, diverting his gaze. I can't see Beranabus, Kernel, Spine, or Artery. I don't care. There's only Bill-E and me in the world now. We're all that matters.

I let magic build within me, then reach out to take Bill-E's hands. I stop. A moment of doubt and disbelief. *I can't do this!* Then I look over Bill-E's head. I see claws coming out of the crack. A massive, shadowy cloud of a face, pure evil. Every shade of darkness imaginable. It fills the gap entirely. I'm not sure what it is — no ordinary demon, that's for sure — but I know it exists only to destroy, and will unless it's stopped.

"I love you, Bill-E," I whisper, my heart breaking. And take his hands.

Magic flows from me into my brother. Soft, warm, pleasing energy. His smile spreads slowly from the warmth of the magic or an especially fond memory. Maybe both. The face of shadows within the crack splits with hatred. It hisses — the sound of a sea boiling dry. Tendrils of darkness dart toward me, a thousand writhing snakes, intent on tearing me away from my brother, separating us forever, using Bill-E for their own evil ends.

"Time to fly, little brother." I sob, and quickly push. The energy touches Bill-E's heart and stops it instantly. No pain. Bill-E's smile freezes in place. The tendrils of darkness blow apart. A furious, hateful bellow as the shadowy face disintegrates. Screams within the crack from scores of cheated demons. The wind stops dead, and the howl is replaced by the noise of rocks grinding together as the crack closes. The screams rise sharply, then die away.

It's over.

I lean forward. Put my lips to my dead brother's forehead and kiss him, my tears dropping onto his still-warm flesh. Then I hug him and Dervish tight, and pray for Lord Loss to kill me swiftly, before I lose my mind to wretched, soul-destroying grief.

# EMPTY VESSEL

✛    ✛    ✛

GROWLS coming nearer, the patter of tiny feet and the snapping of sharp teeth — Artery. I squeeze my eyes shut, silently willing on the demon child.

"No." Lord Loss stops him. "To me."

I reluctantly open my eyes and look up. Lord Loss's face is glowing with sad satisfaction. Artery is making his way to his master's side, glowering. Behind them I spot Beranabus, looking old and frail but triumphant. Kernel is still locked in combat with Spine.

Dervish puts his ear to Bill-E's chest. Listens a few seconds, then raises his face — his eyes are those of a haunted man. "He's —"

"Shut up." I sob before he finishes the sentence. Then, softer, "I had to. Not to stop the Demonata, but for his sake. He would have suffered worse than any of us. They'd have used him. He couldn't have died. He'd have been stuck down here, tormented by demons, knowing he'd handed our world to them. I couldn't let that happen. If there'd been any other way . . ."

Dervish finds my left hand and squeezes reassuringly. We both weep fresh tears.

"Delicious," Lord Loss murmurs, savoring our sorrow. "I wish this moment could last an eternity. It was worth having our plans thwarted. My brethren will break through another time. This world cannot stand against the Demonata much longer. There is a force in motion that cannot be repelled. That is why I pledged myself to the cause of destruction, much as I delight in humanity's enduring pain. Things might have gone badly for me if I'd resisted. But this is the best of both universes. You have done me a great favor tonight. I am almost tempted to let you all live . . . but there are scores to be settled. A few more minutes to relish your agony, then I shall extract my long overdue retribution."

"Yeah, yeah," I mutter halfheartedly, brushing Bill-E's hair back from his eyes. I don't care about the demon master's threats. I don't care about anything except the fact that I've killed my brother and life can never hold any pleasure for me again. Better to die sooner rather than later.

But part of me cares. It stirs in response to Lord Loss's pledge. Energy slides down my arms to my hands. I call it back, but it doesn't respond. It's a strange type of energy, not like the magic I used to fight the demons (*or kill Bill-E*). This is more like the power I felt when I thought all was lost, when I distorted the laws of time and . . .

"We can go back!" I gasp, bolting upright. "We can travel into the past again and save Bill-E!"

Lord Loss hisses, not liking the sound of that. His six arms rise and he glides closer. Laughing hysterically, I bring my own hands up, aim at him, and unleash the energy that has been buzzing at the tips of my fingers for the last few seconds. I expect a huge ball of magic to knock the demon master back, then shoot us into the past, where I can make things right. But the magic comes out in a stream, not a sudden burst. And it doesn't fly in Lord Loss's direction. Instead it flows into Bill-E.

I try redirecting the energy, but I can't control it. The magic seeps out of me and into my dead brother. Lord Loss is watching uncertainly, frowning, perhaps wondering if this is part of a time-traveling spell. Beranabus is dragging himself toward us, not willing to die without a fight. Dervish is still weeping over Bill-E, oblivious to all that's going on.

And then Bill-E moves.

At first I think it's just Dervish shifting the body, but then I see Bill-E's fingers shake and curl inward. His lips part. He shudders. His eyes flicker open.

"What is this?" Lord Loss growls. "Regeneration? It cannot be. I felt his soul depart."

"Billy?" Dervish cries, unable to believe it, falling backward as Bill-E sits up and looks around.

"Bill-E!" I yell with excitement, grasping his arms, squeezing hard, delight taking the place of dread. Somehow I've brought him back. I've used magic to restore his life. Everything's OK. We've beaten the demons *and* saved Bill-E. How's that for a night's work! "I'm so sorry for what I did, but there was no other way. But it doesn't matter now. You're alive. We whupped their ugly hides and . . ."

I stop. Bill-E's looking at me curiously, as if he doesn't know me. And his face is strange. His skin is bubbling, rippling, shimmering, a bit like Juni's did when her face changed. Then he opens his mouth and speaks, and I can't understand a word he's saying, because he's speaking the language of the girl in the rocks. They're *Bec's* words, not Bill-E's.

Lord Loss gasps. "You! No! I will not let you —"

Bill-E's right hand points at the demon master. He shouts something in Bec's language and Lord Loss screeches, "Artery! Attack!" The hell child leaps and Bill-E's hand snaps round. A ball of energy surges from his fingers and Artery explodes into a thousand shredded pieces. He'll never recover from that. The hell-child has been finally, savagely, beautifully killed.

Bill-E stands. His flesh is still changing. The bones seem to be altering too. His eyes and ears. His whole face. Softening. Narrowing. Becoming more . . . *feminine.*

Lord Loss stares at the remains of his dead familiar. Trembles with a mixture of rage and fear. "You should not have come back, girl," he snarls. "This is wrong. You are asking for trouble, and be assured — it will find you."

Bill-E laughs in a way he never laughed before. Catches sight of Spine and waves a hand at the demon — it melts, screaming shrilly, a pool of gristle-speckled liquid within seconds, leaving Kernel to grapple around uncertainly and wonder what happened to his foe.

Bill-E faces Lord Loss again. His face is unrecognizable. His body too — he's smaller and his clothes are hanging loosely on his frame. I'd think I was going mad, but Dervish and Beranabus see it too. Their faces are contorted with bewilderment.

He speaks again, and this time I hear the girl's accent as clearly as I heard it when she spoke to me from within the heart of the rock. Lord Loss trembles, then scowls. "So be it. Perhaps you are right — this is not our time. But it will come, be sure of that. And you won't have to wait another millennium and a half for it!"

The demon master draws himself up straight, then glares at me. "Enjoy your victory, Grubitsch. But remember — the end of the world is coming, and there is nothing you or that apprentice priestess can do to stop it. Remember this also — you killed your brother. He died by *your* hand. How do you think you will sleep tonight? And all the —"

Bill-E barks a short spell. The strips of flesh at the end of the demon master's legs are suddenly alive with rats. Lord Loss squeals, slaps several of them away, then darts to the stalagmite where the body of Juni Swan is impaled. Ripping her corpse free, he cradles her to his chest, snarls hatefully at all of us in the cave, then launches himself at the crack in the rock — now just a thin line a few inches wide. He hits it hard and uses magic to squeeze through. Even so, the walls of the crack scrape much of his and Juni's flesh away, and the rats on Lord Loss's legs are knocked loose. They fall on the floor, turn in puzzled circles for a second or two, then tear away, heading for the surface, back to wherever Bill-E summoned them from.

Except it wasn't Bill-E who made the rats materialize. It was Bec. And I realize, as I watch him looking down at himself, curiously touching his chest and face, that Bill-E's as dead as ever. The girl from the far distant past has taken control of his body and is transforming it into her own.

✣ A couple hours later. Home. Sitting in the TV room with Dervish and Kernel. Kernel is asleep, moaning as he dreams, pain coming at last. Beranabus and Bill-E . . . no, Beranabus and *Bec* are in another room, having a lengthy heart-to-heart. The magician was ecstatic when he understood what was happening. He practically burst with excitement. Hugged her hard, weeping happily, kissing her face. And she stood there, hugging him back, crying too, repeating one word over and over — *"Bran!"*

Dervish and I haven't said anything to each other. He's staring off into space, his face a mess of dried tears. Every so often he shakes his head or makes a soft grunting noise. That's as close as we've come to communication.

I don't know what to feel. I've saved the world from the Demonata, but at what cost? To kill your own brother . . . Nobody should ever have to suffer such a cruel fate. I'm already wishing I could go back and change it. Maybe Bill-E would be better off alive and suffering than dead and gone. Did I have the right to make that choice for him? I don't know.

And maybe I *can* go back. I haven't discussed it with Beranabus yet, but I will, as soon as he's through talking with Bec. Find a way to travel back in time like we did before. Stop any of it from happening. Snatch Bill-E from Juni's clutches. Never open the entrance to the cave. I don't see why we can't. We did it once. I don't care what Beranabus said about waves and trains reaching the end of the line — there *must* be a way to do it again.

✠ Eventually, as the sun rises on a normal day, lighting up a world unaware of how close it came to toppling into an abyss of demonic damnation, Beranabus and Bec return. There's almost nothing of Bill-E left. The girl has taken over completely, remolding his body in her own image. Even his hair has turned a dark red color. One or two small traces of my brother remain — she walks like he did, and her left eyelid hangs a fraction lower than her right — but I'm sure those traits will vanish too.

"Sorry we were such an age," Beranabus says, sitting opposite Dervish. "Loads to talk about. We've cut it short as it is, only covered the more important issues."

Bec stares at the couch, then sits on the floor close to the magician's legs. She looks at me with worried eyes. "I hope you do not mind that I took this body."

I blink. "You can speak our language now?"

"A spell," she replies. "Beranabus taught me. I'm speaking in my own tongue, but it allows me to be understood by others." She sighs. "If I could have worked such a spell when we first made contact, things would have been much simpler."

"I'd normally say there was no point worrying about the past . . ." I begin, but Dervish cuts me off.

"Who are you?" he shouts. "What the hell have you done with Billy?"

"Billy's dead," Beranabus says. "This is Bec, an old friend of mine."

"No!" Dervish yells, lurching to his feet. "That's Billy's body. She stole it. I saw her. I want it back." His hands bunch into fists.

"I apologize, but I cannot give it back," Bec says quietly.

"Even if she could, what would be the point?" Beranabus chips in, roughly but typically. "The boy's dead. Bec took his lifeless flesh and filled it with her spirit. If she vacated it again, you'd only have a dead child on your hands."

"I want him back," Dervish snarls, eyes wild.

"I understand," Bec says solemnly. "You wish to bury him."

"No!" Dervish howls. "I want to hold him and tell him how much I love him. I want to . . ." He breaks down and slumps sideways, sobbing into the cushions. I long to go to my uncle, hold him, help him. But there are too many questions that must be answered. As cruel as it sounds, Dervish will have to wait.

"How did you do it?" I ask quietly.

"Which part?" Bec replies.

"The last bit — taking over Bill-E's body."

She shrugs. "I could see everything that was happening. I came back inside you — when we worked together to bend time, I joined with your flesh and mind. I could have stayed there within you, hidden away, and I meant to. But when I saw what Lord Loss was going to do and realized you wouldn't defend yourself, I had to act. I wasn't sure if I could use the dead boy's flesh. Even if I could, I only planned to inhabit it temporarily — I thought I could possess it, drive Lord Loss away, then leave it again.

"But, to my shock, the body accepted me. More than that — I was able to transform it and re-create my own form. I needn't have — I could have kept your brother's shape — but I wouldn't have been comfortable that way and I don't think you would have been either."

"So this is *your* body now?" I ask. "You're alive after all that time in the cave? Free to grow and live like any other person?"

The girl shrugs again and glances at Beranabus.

"We don't know," the magician says softly, touching Bec's short red hair. "This body might age and develop naturally — or it might not. We'll have to wait and see. Only time will tell."

"Speaking of time . . ." I lean forward anxiously. This was what I wanted to ask about first, but it wouldn't have been polite to barge right in with it. "How did you bring us back from the future?"

Bec shakes her head softly. "I didn't. *We* did it — Kernel, you, and I."

"But you started it. You knew the spells. You were in control."

Again she shakes her head. "It was the Kah-Gash. Although we are parts of the weapon, it has a mind of its own. When we joined, our magic became the magic of the Kah-Gash. It told us how to unite minds and forces. It used us. Like you, I didn't know what it was attempting to do. The time travel was as much of a surprise to me as it was to you."

Bec looks around, staring at the chairs, the windows, the TV. This is all new to her. Unimaginable. She comes from a time when the world was much simpler. She's itching to explore, ask questions, make sense of all the weird shapes and objects. But I can't let this pass.

"Do you remember the spells?" I press. "Could we do it again?"

She thinks a moment and frowns. "It's strange. Normally, I only have to hear something once — I have a perfect memory and never forget anything. But in this instance I have only the vaguest recollection of the spells. I couldn't repeat them."

"You could try," I insist.

She nods. "If you prompt me, I will do my best. But I cannot start without your help. You would have to show me the way, like you did before."

"Grubbs," Beranabus says, "you can't go back again."

"Why not?" I shout. Dervish looks up, startled by the ferocity of my tone. "Why the hell can't I?"

"The Kah-Gash reversed time because the world faced annihilation and there was no other way," Beranabus says calmly. "But it was a massive, perilous undertaking. If it had gone awry, the result would have been chaos, timelessness, maybe the destruction of both universes. You can't take such a risk again, just for the sake of one boy."

"That *one boy* means more to me than all the others in the world put together," I snarl.

"Maybe," Beranabus replies, "but he means nothing to the Kah-Gash. If he did, you wouldn't be sitting here arguing — you'd be spitting out spells, trying to find the energy to take you back. *You* set events in motion last time. You were the first to act. If you want to do it again, go ahead."

"I don't know how!" I howl.

"Ask the Kah-Gash," Bec says. "It spoke to us before and directed us. It's like a person. You're able to talk to it. Ask and see how it responds."

"I don't think —" Beranabus begins.

"Let him," Bec insists. "If he feels he must do this, and if he can, it's not our place to stand in his way."

I stare at her uncertainly, then close my eyes and focus. I search for the magic and quickly find it, an energy and consciousness. There are no barriers between us now. I'll never have trouble finding it again. It's as much a part of me as the oxygen in my lungs.

I tell the magic — the Kah-Gash — what I want. I beg it for help. But there's no answer. I guessed there wouldn't be. Now that we're one, I've begun to understand that other, mysterious part of myself. Beranabus is right. It won't let me smash the structures of time just to save Bill-E.

"Even if you could phrase the spells," Beranabus says as I open my eyes, tears flooding my cheeks, "there isn't a source to track back to. In this time, the tunnel hasn't been opened. There's no river of energy to ride back on."

"We could find another place where demons broke through," I moan.

"No," Beranabus says. "You'd need an open tunnel, but there aren't any."

"Maybe it doesn't have to be open," I whisper — one final, desperate attempt. "We could try a tunnel that's been closed. The energy might be trapped there, held in place, like in a battery or power cell."

"Maybe," Beranabus agrees. "But even if the energy was present and you could unlock it, you'd have to follow the unleashed river of power back to its origin. I doubt it's possible to set limits, to travel back just a day, a week, or a month."

"So what?" I sob. "We'll ride it back to the start and wait. I don't care."

Beranabus smiles softly. "The last tunnel that was anything near to this in size was closed more than three hundred years ago."

"Three . . ." I mutter, feeling the last sliver of hope die within me.

"Let it go, Grubbs," Beranabus says. "Your brother's dead and you can't bring him back. There's no way around it. You'll drive yourself mad if you can't accept that."

"Maybe that wouldn't be so bad." I sigh, then sit there, crying, saying my silent farewells to poor, unfortunate Bill-E Spleen — R.I.-bloody-P.

# ONE SMALL STEP FOR MAN

✠   ✠   ✠

**D**ERVISH'S bedroom. He's sitting on the end of his bed, expression blank. He hasn't washed the dirt and blood from his face and hands yet. I haven't either. Too weary for such mundane tasks. Life will go on, I'm sure — it always does. But right now we're a pair of zombies, capable only of the simplest movements.

"See you later," I mumble, turning to go to my own room.

"Wait," Dervish says. "I don't want to be alone, not now. Stay. Please?"

With a weary nod, I start to pull at the leaves of my magical suit. It's hanging off me in shreds and will be simple to remove. But after picking at a few leaves, I lose interest and crawl onto the bed beside Dervish. I put my arms around him and we hold each other tight. He often held me like this when I first came to live with him, whenever I awoke from a particularly brutal nightmare. But this time the nightmare is reality and there's little comfort to be found in the embrace.

"You had to do it," Dervish whispers.

I break into fresh tears. "He was my brother," I moan. "What would Dad have said?"

"The same thing I'm saying," Dervish croaks. "You did what had to be done. It should have been me. I was his guardian — yours too. The responsibility was mine. But I couldn't find the strength. I failed. If you hadn't been so brave, we'd have all died and Bill-E would have suffered terribly. You did what was best. You should feel proud, not wretched."

I laugh bitterly. "*Proud!* Yeah, sure."

Dervish sighs. "Wrong word. You should feel . . . I don't know . . . maybe there isn't a word for it. But you did the right thing. That has to be enough. It has to keep you going. Because if you let this destroy you — if you let the madness take you — I'll lose two nephews, not one."

"But it's so tempting," I mumble. "I want out, Dervish. I know what it's like to be mad. It's easier than this. Anything's easier than *this.*"

Dervish is silent a minute. Then he says, "I'll make you a deal. If you fight the temptation . . . stay sane, no matter how painful it is . . . so will I."

"You feel it too?" I ask, surprised by his admission.

He nods. By the way he trembles, I know he's not just saying it. "Like you said, anything would be easier than this. But we have each other. If you fight, so will I. I'll stay sane for you if you stay sane for me. Agreed?"

I hug him tighter, loving him more than I ever did before. "Agreed."

Dervish blinks at the ceiling. "It sounds crazy, but I'm sad about Juni too. I know she was evil and I hate her for what she did, but I loved her. I really thought we were going to be together for the rest of our lives. She had to die, and I'm glad I killed her, but . . ."

"I know what you mean. I miss her too. I was surprised Lord Loss took her body. I guess he plans to bury or cremate her."

Dervish snorts. "Eat her, more probably!"

We laugh softly, painfully — the first step back toward something that might one day pass for a normal life. And then, holding each other, we close our eyes, listen to the sounds of the mansion and the world outside, and slowly drift off into a nightmare-laced but nonetheless welcome sleep.

✠ It's dark when I wake. Dervish is snoring lightly. I lie still for a few minutes, enjoying the nearness of my uncle, remembering Bill-E and Loch, my lost brother and friend, trying not to cry, just about managing to hold back the tears.

I ease myself off the bed, careful not to disturb Dervish. My suit of leaves has disintegrated entirely. I brush the last of the flaky patches off, then pad to my bedroom to shower and dress myself in more normal clothes. Thinking about all that's happened while I dress, the night when I almost became a werewolf, the plane, Beranabus, fighting the demons, traveling back through time, killing Bill-E.

Is it just me or does all that seem a bit much for a teenager to have to deal with? Most of my friends have nothing more catastrophic than acne or bad breath to overcome. Wouldn't it have been fairer to spread the craziness around? Couldn't Charlie have been stuck with the werewolf curse, and Frank with being a magician? Couldn't Leon have been betrayed by Juni, and Robbie recruited by Beranabus? And let's not leave the girls out. Reni did her bit, losing Loch, but Mary could easily have had to kill one of her brothers, and Shannon could have done the whole trip through time stuff.

I chuckle (nice to see I still can). I'm being ridiculous, but there's a nugget of truth there. It's been a heavy burden for a single person to bear, especially one as young, inexperienced and . . . hell, let's say it . . . *cowardly* as me. It wasn't fair.

But the universe *isn't* fair. Things don't work out neatly, pain, hardship, and challenges divided equally among those best equipped to deal with them. Sometimes individuals have to be Atlases and carry the weight of the world alone. It shouldn't happen that way, but it does.

At least I have the crumb of comfort of not having fallen. I stumbled and wished all the time that I could bail out. But I kept going. I did what I had to. I came through. It would have been sweet to do it unscathed, Bill-E and Loch alive and well. But in the grand scheme of things, I don't have too much to complain about. That's how Beranabus would see it. And he's right. But that doesn't make me feel any better. The devastation of having killed Bill-E is all-consuming. I don't think any amount of reasoning will ever ease that pain.

Dressed, I go looking for Beranabus, Kernel, and Bec. Trying to focus on their needs, since it helps me not brood about Bill-E. Beranabus was badly wounded in the fight and might need help. Kernel will be in a lot of pain. He said he'd have to go to a hospital. I can arrange that. And Bec . . .

I'm not sure what I can do for a girl who's been dead for sixteen hundred years, only to find herself slap bang in the middle of the modern world. Guide her around the house for a start, I guess. Teach her how to open and close doors and windows, explain what TVs, computers, and CD players are. No . . . they can come later. First teach her how to run a bath and use the shower. Give her some clothes to tide her over until she can go shopping in the Vale. Explain where everything is in the kitchen, what a fridge is, how to open a can, that water comes from a tap and not a well.

I'm padding down the stairs when I hear her. No . . . not hear, exactly. I sense her. In the hall of portraits. Changing direction, I go to check that she's OK. I find her studying the faces of dead Gradys and our various relations, slowly moving from one painting or photo to the next, eyes steady, head cocked slightly to one side.

"These are not drawings," she says without looking around, sensing my presence the same way I sensed hers.

"They're photographs."

"Are they magic? Are people alive within them, their souls trapped like mine was in the cave?"

"No. It's just their image. We use machines to take them."

"Machines?"

"Special tools."

She turns. "I've seen nothing of this new world. I was limited to the cave. I could peer into the universe of the Demonata, but this world was a blank. I don't know what has changed and what hasn't."

"Most of it's different from what you knew. Probably everything. It'll take awhile to get used to, but you'll be OK. Look at it like an adventure — you'll be exploring a brand-new planet."

"Yes. I'm excited. Scared but excited." She sighs, and looks at the photos again. "Your family?"

"Some of them." I move up beside her. "They all caught the disease, or died trying to help others who were infected. You know that some of us change into wolflike beasts, don't you?"

"I saw them in my own time," she answers. "I didn't think the curse would last this long. But I'm not surprised. The blood of the Demonata is strong." She looks at me shyly. "*We* are family. Separated by many generations, but family nevertheless."

"I know."

"The evil priestess — Juni Swan, Nadia Moore, whatever you want to call her — was one like us. Bran told me she could see into the future. Perhaps our demonic heritage was the source of her strange power."

I grunt. I don't want to talk about Juni right now.

"The boy . . . Bill-E . . . he was family too."

"Yes," I mutter. "My brother."

"I'm sorry . . ." she starts to say.

"Don't worry about it," I interrupt. "It wasn't your fault. Bill-E wouldn't mind. He was always keen on recycling."

"'Recycling'?" Bec frowns.

"I'll explain later. Where are Beranabus and Kernel?"

"Outside. They . . ." She casts a look at me and I instantly know what they're doing, what they want of me.

"Already?" I ask stiffly. "They can't wait awhile?"

"No." She looks back at the faces. "I'm not going. Bran told me to stay. He said I would be company for Dervish, that he could look after me and I could look after him. He said we would be good for each other."

"*I'll* be looking after Dervish," I snap.

Bec shrugs. "I'm only repeating what Bran said. He also said Dervish could teach me about the new world, while he could teach you more about magic. In his opinion that arrangement will work best for everyone."

"We'll see about that," I huff, storming off. I pause before turning the corner and glance back at her. "If for some reason I don't return . . . if anything happens to me . . . you *will* take care of Dervish, won't you?"

"I've comforted people who lost loved ones before. There were many in my rath — my village. I will do my best. I promise."

I nod thankfully, then hurry downstairs to sort out things with Beranabus and put him straight on a couple of issues.

✠ The magician and Kernel are in front of the house, squatting in the middle of the road, draped in clothes that they've taken from our wardrobes. They've healed the worst of their wounds, though they're covered in cuts and bruises and Kernel's as blind as he was before. A familiar monolith hangs in the air between them.

"Leaving so soon?" I ask Beranabus tightly.

"Work to be done," he says briskly. "You've seen Bec?"

"Yes. She's under the impression that I'm leaving. Said she'd been charged with the task of looking after Dervish."

"Bec's staying?" Kernel asks, surprised.

"I considered bringing her with us," Beranabus says. "We can't test the Kah-Gash properly without her. I've waited so long to find the different pieces. It might be madness to leave her behind. But the weapon unnerves me. It gave us the power to come back in time and stop the Demonata — but before that it led Grubbs to the cave and initiated this whole train of events."

"I don't recall it leading me," I frown.

"The night you went to the cave when you were turning into a werewolf," Beranabus reminds me. "You cleared most of the entrance. Bec didn't summon you, and Lord Loss wasn't involved at that stage. It can only have been the work of the Kah-Gash. It wanted you to reopen the cave — which makes me assume it also wanted to reopen the tunnel."

"You're saying we can't trust it?" Kernel barks. "After all this time and effort, the things we've sacrificed, the risks we've taken . . . it was all in pursuit of a weapon we don't dare use?"

"We'll use it eventually," Beranabus says. "We'll have to. But I want to study the pair of you first and try to form a better idea of what we'll be dealing with when we next unleash its power. I think it's better not to keep the three of you together until we're sure we can control the Kah-Gash."

"Then why not leave me behind and take Bec?" I ask.

Beranabus sighs. "She's suffered greatly and I care about her deeply. I was scatterbrained as a child — I bet you find that hard to believe! Bec helped me make a vital breakthrough. She set me on track and rooted me in reality. I owe her more than I can ever repay. She deserves to live again, to be human. I'd leave her here forever if I could. That's impossible, but since it makes sense to keep one of you out of the way of the others for a while, I'll gladly give her this free time. As the gods surely know, she's earned it."

"That's the most human thing I've ever heard you say," Kernel murmurs. Then he frowns. "If you knew her, that means you were alive sixteen hundred years ago. I didn't think humans could survive that long."

"They can't," Beranabus grunts. He wipes dried blood from his cheeks, but it's yellow, not red. "You saw me changing in the cave, didn't you?" he asks me.

"I saw . . . something," I answer cagily.

"It surfaces occasionally. Sometimes I need to draw on its powers. It's a dangerous game, involving it so intimately. I run the risk of succumbing to it and losing control. But there are times when we must gamble." He scowls, then says quickly, bluntly, "I'm half Demonata. My father was a demon. That's where my magic comes from. It's how I've lived so long."

"You never told me," Kernel whispers.

"It's not something I'm proud of," Beranabus says acidly. "My mother fell foul of the beast. She never meant for this to happen. It was a horrible twist of fate — or the universe's way of protecting itself from the Demonata."

"Could you have been one of *them?*" Kernel asks. "You've passed for human all this time. Could you have lived as a demon if you'd wished?"

"Aye. The possibility of becoming a full-fledged demon was always there. It still is. My demon half constantly tempts me, urges me to give myself over to evil, join the Demonata, and help them conquer this world. I fight it daily. I've held it in check — so far."

"Which one of them is your father?" I ask. "Lord Loss?"

"Don't be ridiculous," he snorts. "My father was a lesser demon. I tracked him down many centuries ago. I killed the beast and relieved him of his head. Used the skull as a bed-pan for a time." He jerks his thumb at the monolith. "Now that we've had the sordid family history, can we move on?"

"I'm not going," I tell him. "I'm staying here with Dervish and Bec."

Beranabus shrugs. "If that's what you want."

"Don't say it like that. I've done my part. I stopped the demons from breaking through. I killed my brother and saved the world. What more do you want from me?" I scream.

Beranabus doesn't blink. "It's not what I want — it's what the universe wants. And what I've learned from my long years is the universe only ever wants *more*. It doesn't care about sacrifice and best efforts. It needs us to keep fighting. As far as the universe is concerned, there's no rest for either the good or the wicked. I doubt it even understands the concept."

"Well, the universe can go stick its head where the sun don't shine!" I yell. "I'm through. I did what I had to and now I want out, like Bec."

"It's not within my power to let you go or keep you," Beranabus says softly. "Your conscience will guide you. There's no point shrieking at me. It's yourself you should be angry with. If you were selfish, didn't care about the world, or were a tenth of the coward you believe you are, you'd go back inside, return to school, live out a long, happy, simple human life. Which you're fully entitled to."

He takes a step closer, shaking his head. "But you can't, can you? You saw the shadow monster in the cave, the one that almost broke through — their leader."

"It was huge," I whisper. "Powerful. Evil."

"All demons are evil," Beranabus says. "This was different. I'm not sure how exactly, but I intend to find out. I'll track it down, even if I have to visit a thousand worlds and kill a million demons. Normally, Kernel could lead me to it — he's a marvel at finding rogue monsters — but I'm not sure he can pull his weight anymore."

"I might not be able to pull my weight," Kernel growls, "but I can punch your lights out, old man." He bares his teeth. "Or should I say old *demon*."

Beranabus laughs briefly. "Whether or not Kernel can work his magic, I'll find and kill that beast before it discovers another way to open a tunnel between universes. And you'll help me. I know it, Kernel knows it — and *you* know it. That's why you're angry. You don't have a choice because your conscience is directing you. Even after all that's happened — the grief you're going through, the guilt, the fear — you have to do this. You couldn't live with yourself if you didn't."

"Can't we wait?" I cry. "Leave it a few days at least, so I can mourn Bill-E and be with Dervish?"

"The Demonata won't wait," Beranabus says, then smiles faintly. "It's hard for all of us. Kernel needs medical aid. We can build a new pair of eyes for him in the universe of magic but they'll only work in that demonic realm. When he returns to this world, the eyes will soon dissolve. The pain will be awful and will worsen every time he comes back. He can no longer think of Earth as home.

"I want to sit down with Bec, tell her all that's happened in the past thousand and a half years, discuss old times, get to know her again, guide her through the ways of this new and frightening world. Retire and enjoy a few years of peace in her company before my exhausted old spirit passes on.

"But Kernel's ruined eyes don't matter a damn. My pitiful wishes matter even less. We're pawns of the universe. We go where we're needed, do what we must. All else takes second place to that."

"I know." I sigh. "I understand. But Dervish . . . Bill-E . . ."

"Look at it this way," Kernel says softly. "You can mourn your brother here and wait for the world to end — or you can mourn him in the Demonata's universe while you kick seven shades of demon arse all the way to hell." He pushes himself up and walks to the monolith, wincing from the pain, hands outstretched. He touches the dark face of the window, pauses, and lifts his head as though trying to see the sky one last time, even without his eyes and through the layers of bandages. Then, with a soft groan, he steps forward and vanishes.

"I want to say goodbye to Dervish," I mutter.

"No," Beranabus replies, "you don't. That would mean more pain. Better to slip away while he's asleep. He won't like it, but he'll accept it."

"How's he going to explain Bill-E's disappearance to the police, his teachers, everyone who knew him?"

"He'll cook up a good story. He was always adept at making fiction fit the facts." Beranabus extends a hand toward me.

"What about the cave?" I ask, stalling for time. "We have to block the entrance again or the Demonata might —"

"I've already taken care of that," Beranabus says curtly, losing patience. "I've cast spells of warning again, and Dervish will ensure the entrance is filled in as swiftly as possible."

"Your spells didn't work last time," I remind him.

"Because of the Kah-Gash," he snaps. "That has the power to override any spell of mine or any other's. But with you and Kernel by my side, I won't have to worry about that happening again. If demons make another move on the cave, I'll know. Now, are you coming or not? And before you answer, don't forget the Lambs are still after you."

I sneer. "They frightened me once — not any longer."

"Aye. Because you have a more powerful enemy to face now."

I nod slowly, reluctantly, then take the ancient magician's hand. "I'm scared," I whisper. "More scared than I've ever been, and that's saying a lot."

"I know," he replies quietly. "You probably always will be. If it's any comfort, I'm scared too, even after all these centuries."

"How do you deal with the fear?" I ask.

He shrugs. "I fight."

"Is that enough?"

"It has to be."

And on that dubious, dark note, we walk to the monolith, the magician and his assistant, saviors of the world, slaves of the universe. We lay our hands on the smooth black slab. There's a surge of magic. Our heads tilt back like Kernel's did, for one final look at a beautiful, twinkling, star-studded sky. I think of Dervish, Bill-E, all I have to leave behind. The battles to come, the loneliness and pain. I want to run away from it all and hide. But I can't. No — I *won't*.

Beranabus tugs gently. I take a breath, hold it, then willingly step forward with him to face my destiny in the universe of all things foul and demonic.

The horrifying adventures continue in
# DEATH'S SHADOW
Book 7 in THE DEMONATA series

Available now.

THE door to the study crashes open. A wild-eyed Meera bursts into the room. She slips, but grabs the handle and keeps her feet. "We're under attack!" she screams.

Dervish and I stare at her wordlessly.

"We're surrounded!" she yells.

Dervish's face clouds over. "Demons?" he growls, stepping out of his seat, fingers bunching into fists.

"No," Meera gasps. A howl fills the corridor behind her. "Werewolves!"

There's a moment of total, frozen disbelief. Then Dervish grabs a sword from the wall and pushes past Meera. I follow close behind. While Meera hurries to get a weapon of her own, I step into the corridor after Dervish, working on a spell, not sure if it will work — there's so little magic in the air to draw on.

I hear panting. It comes from the far end of the corridor. Something growls and something else yaps angrily in reply. No sight of them yet.

Meera steps out behind us, swinging a mace. She's stuck a knife in her belt. No trace of the gentle woman who was applying makeup a mere matter of minutes ago. She's all warrior now.

"How many?" Dervish asks without looking back.

"At least three. They entered through the kitchen. I'd been snacking. I was just leaving, so I was able to jam the door and stall them. If they'd burst in when I was at the table . . ." She shakes her head, angry and scared.

The first of the creatures sticks its head around the corner. Recognizably human, but twisted out of normal shape. It has unnatural yellow eyes. Dark hair sprouts from its face, and its teeth have lengthened into fangs. They look too large for its mouth — it must have great difficulty eating.

It skulks into the corridor, growling. Long, sharp fingernails. More muscular than any human. Hunched over. Covered in stiff hair. A male. Another two creatures appear behind the first, a male and female. The second male is larger than the first, but follows his lead. His left eye is a gooey, scarred mess. Maybe that's why he's not the dominant member.

As the once-human beasts advance, I step ahead of Dervish and Meera. I try draining magic from the air but there's virtually nothing to tap into. In my own time, these creatures would have been simple to deal with. Here, it's going to be difficult.

The lead werewolf snaps at the female. With a howl, she leaps. I unleash the spell as she jumps. It's a choking spell. If it doesn't work, I won't know much about it — she'll be on me in a second, and I'm defenseless.